Arthur's Pheasant

Colin Seaford

Illustrations by
Lucy Henzell-Thomas

Published by Lord Seaford
Bush Farm, West Knoyle, Wiltshire. BA12 6AE
Tel: 01747 830263

Published 2014

ISBN 978-0-9929053-0-9
Illustrations by Lucy Henzell-Thomas

Printed by FWB Printing Ltd
Bennetts Mead, Southgate Road, Wincanton, Somerset BA9 9EB
01963 33755

This short story was meant to be written to amuse my godsons,
but in the time lapse from writing to printing they have grown up!
So now this tale is dedicated to that marvellous,
beautiful and delicious bird -
The Pheasant and Barry in particular.

CHAPTER 1

November was only half way through and there was a pleasantly mild autumn feeling to the day as Arthur Beamish's guests began to arrive. Today was his second shoot of the season and Arthur was beginning to feel just a little apprehensive that everything should go well. Those he had invited were friends he particularly wanted to enjoy some sport and be entertained by meeting his other guests. It was not a day for mere fun as the late seasons days could be: there were ulterior motives for some of his invitations though no one else was privy to them. He was not a devious man and his ulterior motives were simple and harmless and mostly of benefit to his friends rather than himself, excepting that what enjoyment he saw his guests having was a major reason in staging the whole day in the first place. Peter Maken, Member of Parliament for the southern part of the county, whom he admittedly did not place amongst his friends: more an acquaintance often met, and with much handshaking, had really been asked with the purpose of introducing him to Freddy his godson. Freddy needed guidance and contacts to help in his desire for a political life and who could tell, one thing might lead to another.

Michael Davenport, the Tenth baron of that name, who was a friend and with whom he had much in common even if they did not see each other overly often, was coming not only because Arthur liked him, but in the back of his mind he wanted to effect an unaffected opportunity for his son George to spend some time in the company of Michael's daughter Emma. Had George, or even Helen, Arthur's wife, suspected this, then they would have laughed and poked fun at him for being an old matchmaker even though they too might secretly applaud the plan. The very fact that something like this could be thought of as a plan would surely make it backfire. George had already looked on Emma with moon shaped eyes but being a shy young man was not good at creating meetings enough to cause friendship to blossom. Anyway Arthur had noticed Emma's response and felt the odd nudge could do no harm. There was another thought not to be entirely cast out - Michael had no sons and a lot of land!

Old Ted MacNaughton was there because he was always there, a pleasure to be near him, creeping about with his amazing collapsible shooting stick, bent over with the clutches of arthritis or some advancing back problem and swathed in all manner of bits of cloth. Younger men who offered to help him at stiles only to be rebuffed with mutterings about the far distance of the grave, were astonished at the accuracy of his performance when birds went his way. A performance all the more impressive when judged by the economy of movement employed by this bent old man.

The two remaining guns were relatives, who often cheerily came and to whom Arthur or George just as cheerily returned. A little extra reason for Dick's presence was that both he and Michael bred Simmentals according to their different lights and Angus, a cousin, possessed the leg of a racehorse by the same stallion who was the sire of the whole filly that Peter had pinned his hopes on.

Such were the carefully crafted results of Arthur's invitations and now the sun was coming out intermittently, there was a stiff breeze and quite a lot of blue sky. Could anything be turning out better?

"Well?" said a gravelly voice close to his shoulder. Arthur blinked and came to earth. Old MacNaughton's rather startling blue eyes were twinkling, "Out in the fields already?"

"Yes Ted, and beginning to feel quite excited."

"Good, so am I. Nothing like anticipation to soak up all the wrinkles. The wind is just right for that bit of kale by the Barrow. I'd like to see the boys under the highest ones," he said glancing over to where George and Freddy were - Freddy conversing very happily with Emma as George offered them coffee.

Arthur smiled "How can we get them to draw the right pegs" he replied, his cunning arrangements spilling over.

"That's always a tricky one unless you just don't give us any numbers at all and posts us where you fancy".

Ted always did that. Sometimes not even a stick or marker to be seen, but he always seemed to manage it so easily without any apparent effort and above all without causing anyone to feel anything but that they had been carefully thought about, which of course they had.

"Another drop in your coffee?"

"Mmm".

Arthur's shooting arrangements were old fashioned and mildly formal, numbers and pegs, a line of beaters, no walking guns unless maybe young boys and gamekeeper in charge of all with one of those toneless little reed horns signalling the beginning and end of each drive. At least this way no one had to think about what was going on so there was plenty of time for concentration on shooting presented birds. This was the way he had been brought up in the shooting world and this was the way he felt at home, safe in the security of a known operation with everyone knowing their place in the day and not too much for him to fuss about: Arthur did not like surprises.

"Well George shall we gather ourselves together?" he enquired of his eldest, who had rather abandoned Emma to Freddy and was busy talking to Teal their well covered black labrador.

"Oh yes, right" and he re-entered Freddy's conversation with the purpose of the day giving him the initiative.

"Time to get ready everyone. We'll be walking from here," and out from the house the greenish brown gathering moved, conversation trailing apart as they poked in their vehicles for boots and belts. Now was the time for carefully rude remarks about the accoutrements with which a neighbour adorned himself. Comments on the colour of boots, gaiters, shape of hat, sell by date of gun. The air of excitement and anticipation seemed to release them in a stream, like little boys before some important match and all happy to be brought to order by the referee.

"Now just a word or two about the day"... Arthur gathered everyone in with his eye to mention no 'ground game' and what to do about foxes, he liked giving his little homily not only because by doing so he felt in control but because he felt it was the way all days should start and he did enjoy tradition. So having restored order in his little band they set off across the lawn.

The Beamish house echoed the Beamish character or was it the other way round. A stout edifice built in the time that Queen Anne lurked around the throne. Graceful and attractive, stable and mature, the sort of home to which every Englishman aspires to return after a productive day's work. It was a finely proportioned house with just the right amount of decoration and slender woodwork, between the panes to make it elegant and it gave the feeling of being part of a substantial slice of fertile land from which it drew its nourishment. The trees around the garden, which had never reached maturity in the life time of the original builder's son, stood solid and beautiful in the twilight of their lives. Previous Beamish's had wisely planted replacements which were rising firmly to their task. A large umbrageous oak was filling up the space soon to be vacated by a cedar whose limbs were not as numerous as they had once been, iron rods and struts could only keep the works of storms at bay for so long. A copper beech was spreading across the foreground of a clump of limes who in summer gave the impression of approaching baldness. There was no hurry in their growth just steady change.

Beyond the lawns the group of guns filed through a small iron gate and set off across the meadow towards some rising ground to the west, over which hung a wood of ash and oak with various undergrowth invisible to the guns but waiting enticingly for beaters gathered beyond the rise. They had been there a little while having gathered in the farmyard a short step from the stable yard to the rear of the house. The clock and the Keeper had governed their movements. Sandford, for such was the Keeper's name, was a calm and gentle man with a way with dogs, and as is often the case when a man has a way with dogs he has a way with people. His group of beaters were going to have as much fun as Arthur's guests and be paid for it. They had all been out many times before and knew each other well, fathers and sons; and they had looked forward to today with just as much anticipation as any shooting man, which explained the banter of their conversation now as they waited for the off. Sandford watched from the gate at the edge of the wood drawing on a pipe and keeping himself calm. Not that he was worried, the worst worry was the first day but that had gone well, the birds he thought he had were all there and if a lot hadn't flown much that time this was no cause for fussing. Apart from a young spaniel out for its first season everyone else knew the drill except the pheasants and they would very soon learn, after all he and his beaters were going to teach them and teaching animals what to do was his stock in trade. He was a younger man than Arthur, just turned fifty, which meant he could look back on over thirty years of keepering on the Beamish estate but still the excitement was in him for the day to begin to such an extent that the pipe was useful in spreading calm through him and giving his party the impression that this was always so.

The little party of men with guns were approaching the first of the pegs leaving a trail through the heavily dewed grass, by now anyone with leather boots not well dubbined had a certain dampness creeping in through their socks: walking in wet grass was almost wetter than walking in water. They moved on along the lower ground dropping off as their allotted number showed in the cleft sticks re-positioned the day before. Guns had stood in this valley for years but the pegs were positioned and re- positioned every year. Arthur and Sandford would discuss what took place last time. How two or three birds swung out this way to avoid that ash tree, which was filling out the previous gap, or how the hole where an old beech had gone down in a big January gale caused a small flush to happen just a little early. So back came number one peg twenty yards but that put number four on a bit of a ridge whereas the better sport was down the bank a few yards to elevate any bird another fifteen feet. So the discussion on various positions could go on at every stand. Sometimes, Bill Sandford thought, it was a relief to be out positioning pegs on his own because then he could just let his instinct play without having to voice any reasons. On the whole, though, he preferred doing things together, for that was when he and Arthur behaved as two excited friends, planning the day totally absorbed in the pleasure of what was the culmination of all the previous nine months work. They had known each other long enough to be very much on the same wavelength, and could anticipate exactly what the other was going to say next on the point in question; this made them both pleased that they very rarely disagreed.

By now the breeze could be best described as a fair wind. Hurtling up over the tree tops and making the smaller branches creak so that some of the beaters glanced up thinking the creaks to be remarks made by an irritated squirrel. Bill Sandford produced his little reedhorn and blew a long note, then looking along the line at the edge of the wood waved his stick as a signal for battle to commence.

Down along the meadow the signal had been heard and each armed man became expectant. Peter Maken, M.P., in a rather fetching outfit of lovat green, did a few practice swings at invisible birds, shaking out his shoulders and generally hoping his 'performance' would do him justice. Success was important to his wellbeing; and he dreaded missing the first bird. If he did he knew things would go to pieces, yet if he hit it he could be sure that his eye would be spot on all day and there was nothing like good clean shooting to please one's host - and oneself. Ted had planted himself on his shooting stick and sat taking in the scene without moving, listening and watching. Freddy appeared to have gone into a trance, his gun held with barrels to the sky a bofors gun on the qui vive, all thoughts of Emma wiped from his mind. Whereas George was only too conscious of her since she was standing near him. He was more concerned with adjusting his feet as if taking stance at the crease, rather hoping that no one was going to bowl him a googly. A ridiculous bobble hat marked out where Dick was posed, busily blowing his nose, his empty gun on the grass before him and a large flouncy golden retriever nailed to the turf beside him by a massive corkscrew arrangement.

Arthur's eye travelled on down the row of his guests. He was pleased that Emma had settled to stand by George and hoped she had a firm grip on his son's spaniel Smut. Smut was an energetic hunter, good at it too, but was none to steady as a retriever waiting in the line. He wondered if Ted's dog was asleep as he lay some ten yards out from his master, nothing to worry about with that one. Unlike the shiver of apprehension when his eye rested on the corkscrewed retriever behind Dick!

"Jay!" shouted Angus as high and silent a bird came swooping out from above the trees, Dick grabbed his gun off the ground, fumbled furiously with a cartridge, snapped it up and fired as the offending bird continued its swooping flight out over the meadow towards the next wood! His handkerchief fluttered to the ground - "Damn". Angus appeared to be shaking with amusement.

No time to dwell on this diversion as shouts in the covert proclaimed real action and out came a cock and a hen quite fast and straight, followed by another catching the wind a bit. Peter missed with his first but got the cock up the backside as it passed him, with his second, it tipped and planed down to pitch at the edge of the far wood - "Blast" - and a little blood rose up his neck. The other cock folded up and hit the ground in front of Freddy, who felt awfully pleased. A short pause now for everyone to savour what had just passed and notice that some wood pigeons were on the move above the trees but they swung away.

Down below the trees the beating line was moving slowly and methodically tapping away with sticks and letting their dogs work the bushes just in front. A constant series of little peeps and whistles ensured that none of them ran too far ahead or missed out patches of cover that should have been pushed through. No matter if birds got up and ran ahead, a stop had been placed at the end of the covert and his tapping should turn them back or at least contain them.

"Hi, Hi, Hi!"
"Where's 'ee then!"
"Get in, hi up" – "Forward!" as up went another bird, exploding its way out through the stems, followed by another and another. A productive clump of old ragged robin. Five seconds pause, then a fusillade of shots. Bill smiled, that's what he liked to hear, this was what it was all about.

"Nice and steady please, keep it straight", he called noticing that like him some of his team were responding to the excitement and in their exuberance were pushing on a bit. For a controlled and steady beat one needed patience.

By the time they reached the fallen beech ten or a dozen birds had been flushed, Peter had missed another then joy of joys had shot one cleanly. His damaged confidence had soared back up and he was ready for anything. Ted had a brace on the ground and Arthur had pulled one down that had taken a different line. Two had flown rather low and been allowed to carry on. The line moved on across the clearing, over a strawed scratching area where there was a large feed hopper, into the final third of covert. Here the ones that had run on were skulking back having been turned by the stop tapping on the fence only to hear more whistling and tapping still coming up behind them. This was confusing and rather worrying. Some clapped down right amongst the leaves or crept under the bramble thickets. One or two stood tall craning their necks and peering about. It was one of these, a young cock with the makings of a fine ring on his neck, that started to shout his alarm call. No one took any notice - except the guns in the meadow.

Michael and Arthur exchanged glances. This lovely sound was often the prelude to some explosive action. Nor were they wrong since the inexorable movement of the beaters had come up with this noisy bird, so up he went in a whirring of wings exultant in his own strength, straight out over the top of the trees. Still rising and catching the wind he accelerated way up beyond the wood.

"Bloody hell" muttered Michael as the cock soared out over him. He presented his gun, swung right above and fired twice in quick succession but to no avail. The cock bird sailed on with the wind way over the top of the wood beyond and drifted down to the edge of a piece of kale on the rising ground across the valley.

"That was some bird" called Michael to his host, who nodded and smiled with delight. He was followed by a regular flush and the firing became continuous, everyone concentrating on their own piece of sky. Bird over, up, fire, reload, watching above, hit and remember, miss and forget.

Helen and her sister - Dick's wife, were lurking at the edge of the wood, beyond the line of guns. They were marking what was hit and came on, picking up anything that fell within their orbit equipped with a black labrador, a son of Teal. The latter sat patiently beside his master ready to gather the birds he was marking when the signal came. Picking up behind was fun. Helen enjoyed it much more so when in the company of someone else with whom she could share comments on what went on before them. There was plenty of time for conversation, the view of the whole scene was excellent and yet it was not just a spectator sport for there was a valuable job to be done and the pleasure of working a dog without the tiring work of thrashing about in the beater line. They could see more of who was doing what and how well, than any of the participants, who it was hoped were often too busy. Helen had also learnt to accept the descriptions of how hard that bird was hit, with a leg down and where it was likely to have "fallen". She had found the most satisfactory reply to insistence on these matters was to offer to search thoroughly even though the bird in question had alighted of its own volition to continue its escape on foot, a little puffed maybe, but totally unscathed withal.

The sound of the reed horn keened through the air and everyone unloaded their guns and started to gather the slain in a purposeful way. There were cries of "hi lost" or "Fetch" as dogs were ordered to retrieve birds lying on the open ground twenty yards away which of course they did with pleasure and in doing so gave pleasure. The corkscrewed retriever however, was carried away by the thrill of it all and wanted to transport his burden more than twenty yards so took off in a huge galloping circle. Dick surprisingly, seemed to find this unusual so shouted peremptory orders for his dog's immediate return, which only served to encourage greater feats of galloping followed by complete abandonment of the burden some eighty yards further off. Since this all caused a certain amount of delight to the onlookers enabling them to offer to pick up anything, and since Dick was not unduly alarmed - after all he had shot three - the gathering after the drive became an amusing relaxation after the tenseness of the shooting activity.

An elderly landrover that had been parked over by the other wood served as the game cart as the guns toiled over with what they had gathered and amidst cracks on each others marksmanship the birds were tied and hung up to cool. They then set off along the edge of the wood towards the next ambush. Even in the little time that the first drive had taken most of the dew had dried off the grass with the breeze and glimpses of sun, so when they passed through the gate into the next field no tracks were to be seen. It is amazing how a relatively unorganized group of people can spread out over such large distances in such a short time when all walking in the same direction. By the time Arthur & Dick were through the gate Ted and Michael were over a hundred yards behind so they never saw the elegant fox that trotted across within gun shot of Arthur. Foxes should look their best at this time of year, a new full winter coat, sleek and plump from good autumn feeding, and this fellow certainly did, but what caught the eye most besides his poise and unconcerned carriage was the lack of a white tip to his tail. Where the white hair should have been, this gentleman had black, which gave him a very continental look. He had the air of a rather well bred Corsican bandit.

"Well good morning to you Sir" said Dick raising his hat in salute, "what a magnificent boy that is".

"A black tipped fox" exclaimed Arthur "I wonder if Sandford saw him, he must have been disturbed to come this way now after all the noise we've been making".

At their voices the black tipped fox quickened his pace to a gentle canter then stopped some eighty yards off at the edge of the wood, as they are often wont to do when curiosity overcomes flight, then after a good look he slipped out of sight. Dick and Arthur looked at each other and smiled with pleasure.

Two more drives followed, one from another belt and the other a field of kale, both aiming the birds in the direction of the wood into which the fox had gone for that was their original home wood. The kale was productive and there was heavy expenditure of cartridges. Another dog fox was seen leaving the kale, rather a yellowish animal with a bit of a limp who slipped off up the quiet side of a hedge heading back to the first covert. He was followed by quantities of blackbirds all out for a day's shopping amongst the moist leaves and dark bare earth beneath. The beaters came out of the field, leggings dripping, wet dogs all looking as if they had just been swimming and panting happily with long pink tongues hanging out and lapping with exhausted noisiness at the puddles in the ruts. Bill Sandford's party looked like they'd been working as they lent on their sticks and listened to the next plan. The next drive was going to be a long one. The object was to spread out beyond the big stubble fields lying above a small ridge of downland and walk the fields in towards a clump of gorse and bushes which had been reinforced with a patch of game cover on the topside. By this device they hoped to encompass a covey or two of partridges and project them out over the ridge to the guns waiting below. After that would be lunch and a pint of bitter beer.

Arthur gathered his party and they set off, both groups having quite a long walk to arrive at their positions, there would be no horn blowing since they'd be well out of earshot at the beginning. So without dawdling, away they went. The point of this manoeuvre was to bring them within a short walk of the house and lunch and at the same time catch up with the partridges before the day was too old or something else disturbed them from the stubbles. Helen and her sister took the landrover with Ted and Michael squashed in the back against the rows of the bag, the remainder of the party strode off. Fifteen minutes later they were all lined up at their pegs. Peter wishing he had used the brand new bicycle he had bought with loud proclamations of how "essential it is for one to keep one's body fit in order to have an alert brain." Twice he had ventured out into the city traffic but the shouts of taxi driver and an unexpected shower of rain had rather put him off. He also felt a marginal cretin arriving at the House like an old fashioned postman. The result being that he was feeling extremely puffed in his lovat tweed, some small consolation could be derived from the fact that his host too looked a little the worse for wear. And that was precisely what Arthur felt; a little dizziness was hovering at the back of his eyes and a touch of chagrin at the approach of a senior age when he looked at George and Freddy chattering and laughing. No exertion even noticed. Dick wasn't sweating either but then he had a projectile of some horse power chained to his wrist. No one noticed the cloud of steam as he raised his grey felt hat to let a little wind in. Ted and Michael, of course, were very relaxed and eagerly looking forward to the possibility of a partridge. They didn't have long to wait.

Suddenly and silently black dots appeared over the hill, one hundred and fifty feet up in the air, hardly deviating except for a little whizzing of the wings every now and then.

"Over over!"

Michael's gun flew up. They were coming right above him, one shot forward and swing straight on to another, arching the back, bang, immediate connection. Two birds tumbled down to bounce on the turf. A left and right. There is no way to describe the thrill experienced by such shooting. It is the hunter's instinct honed to a high artistic feeling. A beautiful quarry highly respected, has been mastered by the skill of man using a lovely and elegant weapon; a noble death has been effected. A wounded bird brings shame for other sportsmen will only applaud the high fast clean kill.

More partridges appeared, sailing over further down the line. More guns spoke and two more birds came tumbling down. Little wild grey partridges with brown chest markings and smart eye stripes they fly faster than appearances show with the ability to explode over a hedge and startle the waiting ambusher into missing them altogether. Bill Sandford knew his ground well and presented the birds in just the way he hoped. By spreading his line over all other available escape routes however far apart and all his men coming into view at the same time moving slowly but steadily, they had shepherded the large coveys all the way across the fields not panicking them into taking wing until there appeared to be only one empty quarter - over the ridge. They then followed on into the game crop and bushes to flush another small but steadier covey and several pheasants who had taken up residence on the higher ground.

The small covey had heard the gun fire below and headed by an experienced old cock bird flew the contour of the hill like grouse and made good their escape along the face of the ridge. They flew on for about a quarter of a mile and touched down amongst the thin green shoots of a winter wheat field then ran on a little past the foot of a belt of kale growing along the west of that same ridge. As they scuttled on past the kale stems they were watched by a glossy young cock pheasant with the makings of a fine ring on his neck. After his flight from the first line he was beginning to put things together in his mind. One man whistling in a soft inviting way meant food in plenty, several men whistling and calling in sharp voices with tapping stick noises meant run away. Then there were other men standing with sticks they held upwards and loud banging noises and whooshing sounds when you flew above them. It all meant a bit of a fright but why? He was all right the partridge looked relaxed, they were settling their feathers and starting to poke about for food. It was all rather odd. He had enjoyed the flight having never been so high or so far. Taking off was a bit of a heave but catching the wind under his wings had been really rather exhilarating. In fact he felt terrific, so he popped out into the open stood up high and drummed his wings around him,

"Ya hoo!"he shouted.

The cock partridge gave him a long suffering look and glanced about.

The little horn sounded and the drive was over, everything was gathered up and the whole party wandered off towards the house, over two dozen tired and contented figures.

Michael was ecstatic he was describing to Helen for the second time his exploits with the partridges, she beamed back at him as she ladled stew onto his plate but all the while like a mother hen with chicks she was looking to see who had got an empty plate. The volume of conversation had risen a notch or two in pace with the flow of claret and the increased number of women who now swelled the party. Ted's wife had appeared for lunch and Arthur's two daughters had materialized with the waning of the day; this suited George very well for it took Freddy's roving eye and fast conversation off Emma and immersed him in turn with Anne or Mary. Arthur was very contented looking round the large table, he felt tired and satisfied that all was going well. He reached for his glass to drain it since George was coming round with a fresh bottle, but as he thought he'd got it the glass rolled from his hand and spilt its contents on the table.

"Damn! Sorry"he exclaimed, not much was spilt and Helen brought a cloth

"You clumsy old thing, what did you do?" She looked a little concerned, not over the table but over this unusual lapse.

"Don't know, lack of concentration." The hubbub in the room continued at concert pitch. Peter and Angus were discussing balloting out, Ted was lecturing Angus on the finer points of thatching straw, George and Emma were into Florence and who knew what the others were all talking about but talking they were. Round in the yard adjacent to the back of the house in a large airy room which had once been a coach house, the volume of noise was equally loud, if a little more ribald . The small barrel had a hollow ring to it, the meat pie dish was empty the cake all gone and smoke was beginning to blue in the light above the rafters. The various dogs around the floor were beginning to think they could get away with a little surreptitious foraging, a furtive looking spaniel had already polished off the better part of a cheese sandwich. If he didn't look so furtive he might have got away with it to enjoy at leisure, as it was the owner of the cheese sandwich let out an angry roar which prompted the thief to bolt the whole thing in one gulp. The taste buds of a dog are impossible to fathom. The more they fancy something the less they savour it.

After an hour or more of refreshment the whole ensemble began to make movements for another assault on the woods and coverts. Flushed and loud faces issued out, pulling on boots and coats, scuffling through cartridge bags and generally burrowing about in the paraphernalia that accompanies the back of a car belonging to a shooting man. Arthur and Bill confirmed their plan to go for the kale strip on the ridge. Bill was of the opinion that there had been enough sunshine to encourage the birds to stay out there up to this time of day, The wind was still fairly constant and moving more to the south, so any birds that were there should catch it and fly well as had the partridges during the morning. Arthur agreed with all this and his mind grew excited with thoughts of the afternoon.

They set off across the lawn again back down to that part of the farm that they had left before lunch. The ridge across which the partridges had been driven ran on for some quarter of a mile before turning at right angles into a small re-entrant, it rose at the corner to more than a hundred and fifty feet above the field below which was a fresh looking field of winter barley. The side of the ridge was steep old downland, terraced by the feet of sheep for some hundreds of years, whilst up on the top there was a straggly thorn bush of a hedge with gorse and brambles tumbling out of it and a few stunted ash poking up through various gaps and holes. In the shelter of this was a belt of kale running out from both sides of the angle. The beaters therefore would approach from both ends with a flag waver in the apex and the guns were stationed on both sides of the right angle. Arthur had drawn the peg at the apex of this line, Peter and Angus on his right in line for an escape flight to the sheltered wood behind them. Ted and George were further along. The others lined the re-entrant where escape was across to a hanging cover on the other side. Helen and Rosemary had split up, the latter going up near this hanging woodland where she could best pass comment on her husband's performance and Helen retired across the stream which bisected the field next to the winter barley, to be in line with the larger wood. The stage was set for the grand battue.

The beaters moved slowly close together unseen by the guns below - quite a few birds popped out on foot but the flag waver did his stuff and they darted nervously back into the dark shadows. Far out across the winter wheat the old cock partridge stood on tip toe watching, his family scratching and preening.

Things began to happen, simultaneously a cock took off from either end, shots rang out, three more flew out together, was there safety in numbers? One doubted it and began to climb curling with the wind and ended flying down one half of the line to be brought down right at the end, a corker of a shot by the over excited Freddy whose confidence was now in the clouds. Two hens, a cock, five more on a broad front. Gun fire echoed round the valley. The beaters were getting quite excited and decidedly vocal, cheering a hit, shouting a rise. The ring necked cock had run to the apex confused by sounds on both sides, he looked out into the field and saw the flag waver, "what the hell was that? better not go near him" he thought, so turned and doubled back but the noises, closer now, made him turn again. He stood on the side away from the flag waver with the breeze on his side and the sound of guns somewhere all around and below. Every time one of his brethren took off with a whirr he half crouched to do the same but didn't quite see why he should launch himself when he couldn't identify just where the danger lay. The hens crouched near him. Continuous noise was getting awfully close. Suddenly a voice called out

"Let the dogs hunt this out then".

Almost immediately a big black labrador face was coming towards him down the row of stems "I'm off" he shouted at the hens who both followed suit and he launched himself into the air. Half way through the excited breathless climb everything had become plainly visible he was already going away from the noise but now he saw more men with sticks far below so just kept rising out from the hillside, soaring up he went, all feathers spread. One of the hens crumpled and fell away but he never saw it, besides he was feeling like a king and heading straight out over Arthur. Arthur now finding the whole drive tremendous and the sight of this towering cock filled him with pleasure, up went his gun travelling through the flight-line arching the back as he passed above, fire and connect. The ring neck took one pellet right in the middle of his chest, on the bone, what a shock, he faltered but did not crumple. Arthur crumpled. With a pain like a vice grip right in the middle of his chest. He couldn't set his wings and glide so his gun fell, his knees buckled and he sank to the ground.

He was gliding down, down, gently down feeling numb and laughing to himself. 'Steady on' he thought 'the grounds coming up a bit fast'. Rubbery legs flying, wings flapping, he crash landed on the bracken thirty yards inside the wood.

"Strewth, that was fun" he tried to say but ended up only thinking it, something wasn't quite right with his throat.

Everyone had seen Arthur go down, everyone had seen the cock bird falter but no one watched it fly on, they all ran towards their host who was lying twitching on the ground. Helen ran in her clumsy boots, the sick claws of apprehension clasping inside her. Rosemary ran, she hadn't been a nurse for nothing, there was always urgency. Peter and Michael were beside him on their knees, loosening his collar feeling his pulse calling to him.

"His breathing's a bit fierce. What do you think?"

"Heart attack?" They looked helplessly at each other. Freddy panted up.

"Fetch the landrover, Freddy." Michael said, and he ran on.

George was there, kneeling down "What is it?"

They all gathered. Rosemary recognized a massive stroke.

"Into hospital as quick as possible".

****

"We are a hit baffled Mrs Beamish", said the registrar.

"Your husband has had a severe heart attack and one never knows how far the damage has gone and how much of a recovery can be made. He gives the appearance of being in a coma but every now and then makes some sort of waking noise, which suggests the coma is not very deep. His arms seem to shudder at the same time which gives reason to hope".

Helen and George listened miserably, clutching for straws. But the registrar could offer few. These things took their course.

CHAPTER TWO

Sprawled on a cushion of bracken, Arthur looked around him. He felt totally bemused. This must be a dream he thought and tried to wake up, but his eyes were open already and he couldn't rub them because he didn't have any hands.

"All right, let's be calm about this" was his next reaction "let's test reality a bit." So he shut his eyes and all went black. At least he'd proved they had been open so he looked around. He looked at the fine feathered body which he appeared to be inhabiting one leg felt stretched out so watching the clawed foot at the end of it he tried to wriggle his toes, the long clawed toes moved about.

"Oh Hell" he thought; then out loud - but it didn't come out right, all he heard himself do was give the short alarm call of a cock pheasant.

"Keep calm. Keep calm, must keep calm." Bit by bit he began testing the movements of this unnatural body and the more he fiddled and tested the more natural it all seemed to feel. The field of view was marvellous, he'd never been able to see all round the side of his head before. No hands felt extraordinary but one had this overpowering desire to poke and grab at things with this long mouth-cum-nose. And his feet felt much more useful if not more attractive. The only thing he couldn't get over was the pain in his chest. At least it could be coped with so he stood up and crept through the bracken patch towards the edge of the wood. In the distance he saw the landrover moving about and people standing in a bunch.

"This really must be a dream" he angrily berated himself then pecked violently at one of his toes.

"Ow, ouch". That was extremely sore and he hopped out of the wood to get a better view. The landrover was on the move again and approaching; he started to run towards it. Then he stopped, unsure of himself, a little frightened inside. No one would recognize him but at least they wouldn't shoot him on the ground. The vehicle was only forty yards away, Michael's grim face looked at him from the passenger window. As it passed he saw Helen look out from the back where she was bent over a figure on the floor. Arthur was desperate, he shouted out her name running after her but it came out as a triumphant crow and a drumming of wings. Everyone just looked at him, including the main shooting party on foot who were all following in the wake of the landrover.

Why did they all look at him like that, stolidly staring and then making comments to each other obviously about him. It was really very embarrassing and infuriating - they were his friends, his guests - his family! His dog! Teal was trotting towards him with his tail up and a line of hackles risen along his back. He had not got into the landrover because his master didn't seem to be there and now here was this cock pheasant that was looking at him in a queer way and reminding him of his master. Arthur crowed again drumming his wings in fury and mortification at not being able to communicate or be recognized. Teal growled and started to run. Arthur turned and fled and someone whistled at Teal.

Back in the cover of the wood Arthur raged inwardly with the dawning of what appeared reality. His erstwhile human friends were gone from sight and the quietness of the countryside settled back. The awful thought that he'd got to make the best of it overcame his anguish, for how long? Maybe it would all come right in the end; maybe it wouldn't so he began to feel miserable. He sat on the root of a tree, hunched his shoulders and moped. For two hours he wallowed in his discomfiture and the afternoon turned to evening.

Suddenly there was a soft tread and a bright eye was looking at him. A hen pheasant had stepped up the bank towards him and was having a good look first with one eye then bowing and turning to check him over with the other. She made a little cheeping noise and seemed to be asking him if he was all right.

"No I am not all right", he tried to say "some bloody man shot at me and here I am." She continued looking interested and compassionate so he roused himself from his hunched position, it would have been churlish not to, and tried to say thank you for asking - his reply came out pretty near to what he wanted in the form of a sort of cooing sound. This pleased her and her demeanor then seemed to infer that she thought he was a fine specimen of a fellow and was happy to make his acquaintance, he surprised himself by thinking that indeed she was a charming creature herself and he would be happy to walk a little with her. So they picked their way across the woodland floor together, she stopping and looking around every few paces he following and finding himself watching and looking.

Two more hens approached under the bare hazels, rustling the leaves as they trod. They seemed to know his comforter and were converging on a group of larch trees a little way off. He knew those trees well, after all hadn't he planted them shortly after he left school? And now it looked as if they were all going to go to bed in them! With the fading of the light Arthur felt within himself an urge to get up off the ground into the safety of a tree, there was potential danger on the ground, the urge was fuelled by a definite apprehension. One of the hens crouched then launched herself up into the larch tree above her and after a bit of peering about the other two followed suit. Arthur looked up at them then around at the under-growth. '1 suppose I can still fly' he wondered

'Don't want to make a fool of myself in front of them'. His arms felt ready despite the stiffness across his chest so he sprang into the air and whirred them about and low and behold he shot up into the larch tree right past his friend where he made an undignified clatter of a landing on the branch above. His long toes held the branch firmly. 'Well, well, well, this isn't so bad'. He shuffled a little closer to the main trunk and sat down feeling surprisingly secure and at ease and listened to the evening noises of the woods. Whisky and a log fire were a long way off, nor did he particularly want them, it was conversation that he wanted most, he did feel awfully empty and alone.

Sleep came with darkness, for not only was he mentally tired but the body he now found himself inside was physically tired after the days flights not to mention the thump on the chest. The wind had died down as evening drew on and a fine still night followed with plenty of stars visible; a rather cold and heavy dew settled.

****

In the intensive care ward of the hospital, lights glowed round each bedside, monitoring screens blipped and all the paraphernalia of life support hung round each patient as their bodies struggled to survive. Helen was sitting by Arthur's bed rather numbed by all that had happened but just wanting to be near him. She held his finger tips but in a strange way felt he was not there. The figure lying there in complete repose infested with tubes and little bits of tape was but the shell of her husband and she found herself looking at him in a detached way wondering how deep inside was the real Arthur and would he please please return.

George and Anne came softly over from where they had been having coffee and talking to the nurse.

"They suggest we go home and rest ourselves now", George said "Daddy is quite stable and could be like this for quite a long time. They've promised to phone if there is any sign of him coming round."

Helen patted Anne's hand on her shoulder "I know, I know."

"You'd only get sleepier and sleepier and then you won't be able to be useful" Anne whispered, "It's after eleven now".

They all went quietly out down to the car outside which was pearled with the moisture of a cold dew, and drove home through the dark countryside.

****

With the dawn came general activity in the woods as all the day people started to wake up and make a noise about it. The night people tended to be rather quiet by comparison which made the decibel level of the dawn chorus all the more startling. Arthur awoke feeling somewhat stiff but not at all cold which surprised him. The few times he had been out all night clothed in an army great- coat he had felt the cold creep insidiously in however he positioned himself. This morning looking at his feathers, they were beaded with damp but he felt as warm as toast. He scratched an eye and peered below, the hen pheasant on the branch below looked up perkily and made a little noise which he took to mean "good morning and how are we today then?" His attempt to articulate a charming response came out as a gruff coo but it seemed to please her.

A wood pigeon three trees away was being particularly deafening. Arthur wished he'd shut up and fly away; he found he was much more interested listening to the smaller birds lower down through the wood. A robin proclaiming his importance from a spindleberry branch a blackbird further off doing a quite delightful virtuoso from a clump of elder. Their songs were not only beautiful they told him that all was peace on the groundfloor. Long horizontal shafts of sunlight began to play around the branches as the cold grey dawn light gave way to day. A roe deer barked somewhere towards the end of the wood. He cocked his head and caught the hen's eye again. They shrugged, 'barking at his own shadow', he thought.

The other thought that crossed his mind was that he was feeling rather peckish and that since he felt that his predicament was not a dream but reality, he was surprised at the equanimity with which he seemed to be accepting the situation and actually was relishing the thought of some wheat or kibbled maize for breakfast. It even occurred to him how nice it would be to find an earthworm. Counteracting this attraction he imagined a plate of bacon and egg, but was startled to realize that the earthworm was more desirable!

These thoughts on the realities of the situation required action, so he straightway launched himself off the branch aiming at an open grassy patch and having landed rather smartly exactly where he wanted to be strutted around looking for something edible. Both hens followed him down and began making their way cautiously towards the ride that ran along the bottom of the wood. He followed in a more upright fashion. Stepping out onto the ride he saw what he wanted, a worm. Wallop and down it went followed by a few sips from a puddle in the ruts.

This little morsel had quite stirred up the pangs of hunger so it now seemed frightfully important to do some serious foraging. Bill Sandford had set up a feeder midway along the ride back in September with straw scattered about and branches cut back to let in the sun. It was to this area that the three of them steadily progressed, nor were they alone. On rounding a bend in the ride the feed area became apparent and dotted about over the straw were some twenty other pheasants. It was a popular feed ride, for it was sheltered from all sides except where the sun was rising and made a very attractive breakfasting area. However it was the presence of several other cocks that was causing Arthur some hesitation. He felt rather antagonistic towards them. His two friends darted on towards the feeder so he made the best of it by drawing himself up and walking sedately after them. The first of his brethren to be encountered looked very common or garden and a fair bit smaller and it immediately deferred to Arthur by moving out of his path. A larger darker cock bird was pecking at the feeder and the two hens had taken advantage of this by gathering up the grain he spilt. Arthur quickly joined them, being overcome with a pang of hunger. He had hardly picked up three grains when he suddenly received a severe peck on his back.

“Ow” he sprang away and turned to face towards whoever had pecked him. The large dark cock was not pleased at all but made a quick dash and pecked him again.

“Get off” shouted Arthur and ran back a few paces. He found he didn’t have the nerve to take counter measures. Being pecked was sore and he didn’t want any more pecks, besides this bird was bigger than him. It seemed to have an arrogant determination which he felt in no way able to match. This unseemly little episode was rather delaying breakfast, so he peeked about in the straw while waiting for the feeder to be available. A few minutes later the dark cock wandered off apparently satisfied. Arthur stepped forward; but another bigger bird than he had been waiting too and so he felt obliged to wait again. This was tiresome. His lady friends had found enough and giving him sidelong glances were moving off to a corrugated shelter for some dusting.

Arthur felt miffed and embarrassed, he was still hungry and had been belittled in front of them, he ‘wasn’t going to let any other sodding cock put him off his breakfast’. Swelling with anger and not a little flushed with shame he went right over and peeked the cock who was monopolizing the feeder quite hard on the rump. It worked like a charm. First lesson in aggression - be determined.

“Dear me, but this is all so different” he mused “politeness to women is still the norm but manners and men don’t mix!” Next move was to sample the delights of a dust bath. The two hens gave him coy looks and one backed out of his way. He merely accepted that as a friendly gesture and settled down where she had been to start fluffing his wings and scratching up the dry dust and litter. Actually it was all rather a pleasant sensation like having a shave and putting on talcum powder all rolled into one. He shook himself in a cloud of dust and felt ready to face the day.

With his immediate physical needs catered for Arthur’s worries returned. He couldn’t just let this state of affairs be. Something had to be done and the first thing to do was to go home and find out what was happening and try and explain where he was. The two hens were not all that bothered about his presence and only spared him a glance or two as he set off along the ride towards the end of the wood.

"How am I going to explain" he thought. "I know what I want to say but it just doesn't come out in words. No one's going to believe me unless I speak." There didn't seem to be an immediate way round this problem; better to put it aside and concentrate on getting to the house. Funnily enough, although Arthur was quite aware that he could fly, something in him preferred to undertake the journey on foot. To fly was to expose oneself and the landing area may not be all that safe, on foot he could spy out the ground better. The first meadow was devoid of life, nevertheless he approached the gate into the next field with caution, slipped under and stepped slowly forward looking to left and right. He was just clearing his throat in an attempt to say something polite to a buck rabbit out nibbling the grass when "whoosh" - the rabbit thumped and pumped, a rushing of wind and a grey something whizzed inches from his head causing Arthur such considerable fright that he squawked aloud, lost his footing and deposited a dropping all at the same time. Thoroughly ruffled and not a little scared he gathered himself together realizing that it was a hunting sparrowhawk that had upset him so as it dived along the hedgerow trying to surprise small birds into becoming its breakfast.

"Surely it wouldn't have gone for me?" he asked himself. "Don't count on it" came his own reply. This seemed like a real problem for how could one protect oneself from sudden attack from the air. If he spent all his time keeping his surroundings under surveillance for possible dangers there would not be time for anything else. One simply had to accept aerial attacks in the same light as being run into when out motoring, it happens to some but not many and there's always that risk.

An hour later he'd covered the mile from the feed ride to the edge of the garden and was standing by the metal fence under the cedars looking across the lawn at his home wondering what to do next. Everything was quiet, a thrush was hopping about on the lawn, nobody - no human body was visible or to be heard. Arthur walked across the lawn with some trepidation.

“It’s time to put these croquet hoops away” he mused. Between the house and the lawn was a flagstone path widening into a sort of terrace in front of the drawing room whose tall Georgian glass doors looked out across the parkland to the downland away to the southeast. By now Arthur was on the path but couldn’t see in over the windowsills so he walked along to the drawing room door. Inside the house he heard the hall clock strike ten. Peering through the doors he couldn’t see a soul and was about to go on round the house and try the kitchen when his daughter Mary appeared crossing the hall. Mary had only just arisen and was tottering down for some coffee but as she crossed the hall she glanced through the drawing room and noticed a cock pheasant outside seemingly peering in. This was rather unusual so she went through the room towards it. But it just stood there looking at her. She wasn’t really sure it could see her through the glass so she bent down and tapped on a pane. Far from being frightened it just seemed to swell its feathers a bit and opened its beak as if about to say something.

“You lovely thing” she said and unlocking the door she opened it. Arthur was ‘gobsmacked’ He kept opening his mouth. Mary was smiling at him only a few feet away.

“Hello you pretty fellow” she said, “who have you come to see?”

“You!”, shouted Arthur and out came a loud crow, which made them both jump. Worse, it brought Teal rushing out of the kitchen where he had been lying in his basket, running straight at Arthur. It was too much. Arthur took off shouting at Teal to remember who his master was as he flew over the lawn and landed at the far end of the herbaceous border. Teal stood there wagging his tail somewhat puzzled. Mary was scolding him and yet he felt rather happy; Mary could still see the pheasant standing amongst the brown pruned clumps of herbaceous plants and he still seemed to be looking at her, but lest Teal run off she closed the door.

A black mood descended on Arthur in the flower bed, his neck sunk his shoulders hunched and feathers puffed out. He slumped there in misery and resignation. This was awful, he didn’t know how to cope and for half an hour he just wallowed in depression. But nature does not allow perfectly healthy specimens to wallow for long. Little pangs of hunger began to assert themselves reminding him what life was really all about - living.

“Oh well” he sighed to himself, “now where is the nearest easy meal - apart from in the house!” Bill Sandford’s newest feeder was in a shelter belt of pine and oak trees down the drive past the stables, on the other hand in the stable yard was Bill’s feed store. The door was usually open to allow cats easy egress. Here would be a sumptuous feast in double quick time as long as there were no dogs lurking about or even maybe a cat. Arthur wasn’t sure how things would go if he came face to face with a cat. Still if he went that way and the coast was clear all would be well, if not he’d go on to the shelter belt and take his turn at the feeder.

The stable yard seemed empty, at least Bill’s pick-up wasn’t there so there shouldn’t be a dog about. Arthur went cautiously into the yard, the door was open and he could see the lid on the bin was up. A small party of sparrows had discovered this too and were having a high old time, which encouraged him considerably, so he boldly walked into the feed store. Pausing a while just inside the door to become accustomed to the dark interior he had a good look round. The sparrows chattered excitedly as they feasted. Arthur sprang up onto the bin, which he knew contained kibbled maize, it glowed up at him and he laughed inside with delight. His internal arrangements told him that without a doubt this was exactly what they wanted, so down he hopped and started greedily to fill himself up - Oh boy but this was good! The black mood was well and truly banished in a feeding frenzy of pleasure. So occupied was he with stuffing in the maize that he didn’t notice the sparrows had departed but then suddenly there was the sound of human feet out in the yard.

“Damn and Blast” thought Arthur “Is there no peace?” He crouched ready to jump up onto the rim of the bin. The feet approached and before he had quite launched himself - for he lost balance through his extra weight and the loose footing of the grain - an arm came across and shut the bin above him. All was dark as pitch. Noises continued in the feedstore and the feet went away.

Various expletives ran around Arthur's mind but he could not vent them to the world at large. The only relief obtainable was to scratch the wall of the bin viciously followed by a good peck. It was only just midday, was the arm going to return and open the bin today? Probably not since all the feeding took place in the morning. This was intolerable. He needed some grit and a good drink would not come amiss. He couldn't just sit there until tomorrow. Arthur launched himself in the direction of the lid, hurt his head, scrabbled for a foothold with his feet and fell back on the grain below panting. There had been no give in the lid but he had located the feel of things so he tried again, no go; and again and again. Exhaustion left him sprawled with wings out, several broken feathers and a grazed head with nothing to show for it. This was just too much, every move he made seemed to end in humiliation or disaster. "This is simply not fair" he whinged within and sat sullenly in the darkness waiting for release.

****

While Arthur was sitting glowering in the feed bin Helen and Anne were returning from the hospital where they had been most of the morning. There had been no change in the patient lying in intensive care, in fact he seemed quite stable but the registrar had been sufficiently puzzled by one or two visible symptoms that were not normally to be found in similar cases and he had asked a cardiac specialist to inspect the patient and pass an opinion. This eminent gentleman with soft limpid hands and the far away look of the expert in his field had pressed and prodded, tapped and listened. In the privacy of a consulting room they discussed their puzzlement.

"There is no doubt that he has had a massive stroke and is in a precarious state, on that we are agreed. The treatment he is receiving is correct for this diagnosis and we are holding him stable. I cannot give a reason for the muscular spasms in his arms and epiglottis nor can I give an opinion on the discolouration in the patient's eyes." Limpid Hands had summed up the situation as the Registrar had described it to him before he had inspected the patient. The Registrar knitted his hirsute brows and nodded.

"Looking through his medical history is not helpful either, no hint of Parkinsons, no sign of tremors, no Malaria"...

"Yes interrupted Limpid Hands "that faint yellow ring effect in the eye is very interesting. It could well have been developing in the patient well before the stroke and only become noticeable as a result, I see no connection with the stroke as such. It is strange, certainly, almost bird like."

Beetle Brows nodded and 'hmmd'. They stood lost in thought for a moment. "Would you care to talk with the patient's wife, she's been waiting to see you?"

"Certainly, certainly." They went down the passage into another room, light and airy with a view over the town roofs, where Helen and Anne were waiting.

Having heard what the doctors had to say and having endured their sympathetic glances Helen spent some time in her husband's room while Anne popped off to do some shopping before joining her mother, then after a little while they decided to go home. Back at the house they hurried around putting some lunch on the table though if either had been left to their own devices neither of them would have had more than a cup of coffee. The same went for Mary but because they were together they indulged in a little sociable picking and nibbling. Mary recounted the incident of the cock pheasant earlier in the morning.

"The funny thing about it all was the way he kept looking at me and opening his beak, as if he was trying to tell me something" Helen frowned and Anne rather reduced the significance of the last remark by saying that "It was probably addressing its reflection in the window and you came along and gave it a fright, poor bird!"

****

The 'poor bird' was getting thoroughly cheesed off with his situation. He had walked around working out the size of his position, he had jumped up and down to firm up a launching pad for the moment of release, but neither of these activities took very long. Arthur had no idea of the time; sounds only filtered in in rather a muffled fashion. From time to time in this timeless zone he heard a vehicle and braced himself for action but no footsteps followed, no other noises of life without. On the other hand he didn't want to go to sleep and be surprised and maybe caught, the only sure escape was immediate flight or soon as the lid was lifted when he would have the element of surprise. Bemoaning his situation didn't help much. He began to recite poetry to himself. He even got as far as reciting 'A father's advice' on shooting but rather choked on the irony of the last two lines

"All the pheasants ever bred
Won't repay for one man dead."

He remembered stressing these two lines to George when he had required him to learn the poem before being allowed to handle his first airgun, even though at the back of his mind was the nagging feeling that, if the truth be known, he rather felt that there were a number of his fellow men that were not worth a brace of birds, let alone all 'the pheasants ever bred!' Now his feelings were rather mixed. He had never been an anthropomorphic sort of fellow. Always regarded creatures with respect, with wonder: even loved some, Teal for instance, but they were only creatures, many were edible and quite right too. Nature was nature because some members of creation lived by devouring others. Pheasants ate grain and foxes ate them and everything reproduced to keep the whole cycle going. From his present position his views were not really changed, he had already discovered that there was no 'civilisation' of the creatures, he couldn't even converse with the pheasant he had met, he could only make noises and gestures indicating basic wants and feelings. Arthur had the knowledge to improve their lot but he knew that he could no more organize a gang of pheasants to kill a fox than he could explain to his daughter that the resplendent bird on the terrace was her father. This train of thought was worth pondering further but only as a side issue, his main line of thought should be on how to get his message over to his family. 'Where was his human body?' Of course! how obvious; it was no good making messages for other people, he'd got to find himself

..... Then what? Well then at least something might present itself. At least Arthur had arrived at a decision on the first step.

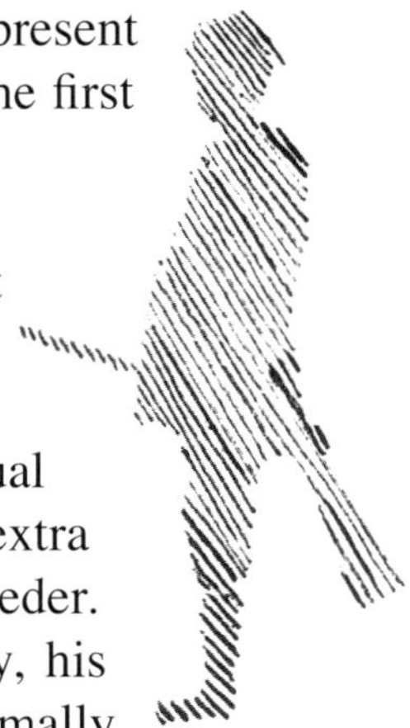

Obviously nothing was going to happen until he got out of this bin.

Bill Sandford had checked round his feed rides as usual that morning, in some he whistled and scattered extra wheat and maize, in others he just checked the feeder. There was no reason not to do his tasks normally, his employer would expect everything to carry on normally however ill he was. The next shoot was three weeks away, plenty of time to cancel or make other arrangements when they would all know more about the situation. Yesterday had been rather awful. A good days sport no question of that everything had gone frightfully well until Mr Beamish had collapsed. The awfulness was the sudden change from happy enjoyment to miserable worry and fear. Here was a man who he admired and respected, with whom he enjoyed friendship, for whom he had worked all his working life more than twenty five years. Now suddenly thoughts of the future crowded in when they had never been entertained before. He had known George since he was a baby in a pram and was extremely fond of him but that didn't necessarily mean the Sandford future was secure. Unknown factors could come into play if Arthur Beamish died, outside financial matters could change things, who knows? Certainly Bill knew nothing of future plans for the next generation so not only did he worry for the health of his employer as a friend he feared the unknown possibilities of the future for himself.

But with a life like his Bill couldn't worry long. He only had to look down a feed ride dotted with birds scratching the straw, framed by the trunks and undergrowth of the surrounding woodland for his spirits to lift and a smile of the pleasure of living to light up his face. Midday found him putting out a little fresh straw on the ride in the shelter belt near the drive. Glancing up the drive he saw a stoat run across the gravel and dart off up the hedge towards the back of the stable yard. The gun was in the pick-up, always handy but some fifty yards away. He quickly fetched it then just as quickly made his way up the grass verge to where the stoat was last seen. Bill was not fond of stoats in the middle of his patch. He stealthily followed the hedge keeping an eye on the drive in case it popped out his side. At the gate at the back of the stable yard wall he climbed up and leaned over; not a sausage.

"Cunning devil", he said with admiration, and stood watching a while in case the cunning devil belied its name and should appear again. Then hearing the twittering of sparrows over the wall in the yard he remembered he'd left the feed bin open again so went quietly round and shut it. Still no sign of the stoat when he stepped silently down the drive.

"Oh well, we'll keep an eye out for you," Bill muttered and returned to his tasks.

George came and found him later that afternoon, as he was scrubbing out the kennels, and told him the news on Arthur's condition. They talked quite a long time and dusk was falling when they parted. George to return to the house for a cup of tea then off to the hospital and Bill to finish off the kennel, feed his dogs and then prepare himself some sustenance. Bill's wife had died the year previously from cancer so he now lived alone if one can be described as being alone with six dogs, two cats and a tame magpie. No one knew if he was lonely for he was a solitary man, though always very easy and sociable when people were about; only Bill knew the moments of darkness that beset him from time to time. One such moment came upon him that evening when he had gone indoors, so he just stoked the Rayburn and sat beside it staring into the glowing coals while his magpie hopped around the room eyeing him speculatively, wondering at his inactivity, but having sufficient fellow feeling to recognize when silence was appropriate.

Next morning he awoke bright and refreshed and looking forward to the day even though it had yet to dawn. He fussed around the cottage doing the things that should have been done the evening before, then out to tend the kennel dogs before having some breakfast. Half an hour later he drove the pick-up into the stable yard to collect a couple of bags of wheat and a bucket or two of kibbled maize. The maize was well worth adding to the ration as pheasants seemed to show a particular fondness for it which encouraged them to remain in the vicinity of the feeders. So taking up a paper bag he opened the bin. The unexpected is often a jolt to the system which is the great advantage of the element of surprise to the "surprisor". Bill certainly received a shock as a cock pheasant exploded up out of the bin with a cacophony of noise and slapping of wings and flew hurtling out of the doorway.

"Well, bless my soul!" would be a reasonable interpretation of the words that issued forth.

Arthur made a very untidy landing in some Michaelmas daisies which lined one of the paths in the walled garden. He intended to land on the path but being somewhat dizzy had veered into the woody embrace of a purple clump. He had been sort of sleeping when he heard the pick-up outside and the sounds of movement in the feed store getting closer, so he had immediately crouched in what he thought was the right spot for take off. As soon as the lid opened he just went, blinded by the light or not. It was a fearful scrabble but he could see the open door and drove himself out and up over the stable roof. That's when the dizziness struck him and a landing had to be made. What a relief though; he was out and free again, with fresh air and daylight all around. My hat, how thirsty he felt. There was a low stone trough by the greenhouse which would be full of cool clear rain water so he scuttled over there, a bit wobbly but everything was coming back to life quickly enough. After a delicious drink a bit of foraging seemed in order and there were quite a lot of tasty bits and pieces in the garden. Forty minutes later he was quite recovered and a varied breakfast had been consumed, worms, slugs, loganberries (rather old and musty), a variety of seeds, half a rotten potato and a small piece of digestive biscuit near the potting coach-house. Now to pursue his plan which had been given much consideration in the feed bin. First step was to fly up onto the stable yard roof and walk along the ridge to where he obtained a good view of the front door and the upstairs windows on the east side, one of which was his bedroom. The front door and all the north facing windows were firmly closed but their bathroom window was open a bit at the bottom. Being a sash window, that meant landing on the windowsill and passing in should be quite easy as long as he could brake sufficiently before impact. A pheasant landing usually requires a short runway to maintain equilibrium so it struck him that the safest way to alight on the windowsill would be to launch from below and aim at it as if it was the branch of a tree. The only visible activity anywhere around was an industrious group of starlings on the lawn below the window, no sign of anyone inside the house. So he sprang off the ridge and glided down to the grass. The starlings flew away annoyed by this intrusion. Arthur stood there warily waiting in case he had been seen then walked forward to stand below the window. A few more glances around and up he went. A bit of scrabbling about on the sill for there was nothing much for him to get a grip of: a quick hop and he was in the bathroom.

Feeling a bit nervous now he could not stop himself depositing a dropping on the thick white pile of the carpet.

"Oh dear!" he sighed "Too bad."

All was quiet and the bedroom door was partially open. With nerves stretching even tighter he peeped round the door. Helen was sitting on the bed looking at him. She was dressed and had been writing a letter but had heard his entry in the bathroom and was wondering what it was. There was no one in the other half of the bed. Arthur stood transfixed looking at her and she just looked back in wonderment. He stepped slowly forward into full view and stopped again. Nothing was said, there was nothing to say. A minute passed. Then footsteps on the landing and George asking his mother if she was ready to go to the hospital and the wretched Teal trotted into the room. For the second time Teal broke the spell. He woofed and bounded forwards. Arthur fled back into the bathroom and sprang out of the window to alight back on the lawn.

Looking back up he watched George throw up the window and look out, Helen was looking through the bedroom window. Neither of them said anything they just watched him in puzzlement not without a tinge of awe. Arthur didn't quite know what to do, so mustering as much dignity as he could he walked slowly away across the lawn.

He was troubled now. Plan A had been a wash out. His other self must be in 'the hospital', whichever one that might be. Or was Helen going for some reason connected with herself; hardly, he thought. Arthur spent the rest of the day in the far reaches of the garden. He foraged about, inspecting the flower beds and shrubberies with more detail and thoroughness than ever he had done before. At one stage by a clump of laurel he came face to face with another cock pheasant who bristled with a proprietorial air and threatened him.

"Not bloody likely" thought Arthur "No one's going to tell me to clear off in my own garden, least of all some wretched piddling cock pheasant!" And he rushed upon the other bird with furious indignation springing in the air and buffeting him with vigour. It was enough: his claim on the territory was established and the other bird ran urgently away to conduct his business elsewhere.

Feeling in no way pleased with what he had done Arthur strutted about in an anger of indecision. The day was beginning to fade rather coldly; the mistle thrushes clucked above as they flew by. The blackbird who had been hopping round the borders all afternoon sounded his evening alarm call and flew off along the clipped yew hedge at the back of the herbaceous border. Pigeons were heading for their roosts, swinging across the parkland on well used flight lines. The bullocks below them, which had been resting for the past two hours, had all got up and were steadily grazing away at the coarse tired grassland. Everyone seemed occupied and busy. Arthur fidgeted and tried to decide where he was going to spend the night. There was a small plantation of Norway spruce at the back of the walled garden which looked rather inviting and out of the wind. He rather sensed that it was going to rain later and the wind was rising as well, so he started off in that direction.

Things were really quite cosy in the middle of the plantation half way up a spruce tree. There was the sound of the wind outside but not a breath of it deep amongst the branches, which made the sense of warmth and safety all the stronger. A number of other birds had also chosen this for their roosting place. Arthur counted over a dozen sounds of roosting birds rising into the trees and there must have been some he missed, like the silhouette in the next tree which was there before his arrival. A plan for the following day was beginning to form in his mind. He was convinced now that a confrontation with his alter ego was the only hope of somehow redressing the balance. The problem seemed to be locating himself and not knowing the state of play wherever that self was. There were three possible hospitals where a sick gentleman such as himself could have been taken, each in a different direction and each a long way off as the crow flies, let alone the pheasant. He ought to put himself somewhere where he could hear family conversations but not put them all off by being seen by anyone. And that went for Teal too, his lovely dog over whom he had no control at all. Taking this plan further meant going to the hospital, entering the place and finding the right ward or room and doing all this unobserved. Rather a tall order. Pheasants aren't normally seen strutting along the corridors of hospitals, National Health or Private. He couldn't just don a white coat and become inconspicuous, he was more likely to become someone's lunch. What if he was wrong about the whole thing and Helen had just been going for a check up. What if there was no other self any more. Arthur shivered and sunk deeper into his feathers. At the edge of the plantation an owl gave a speculative hoot. He had simply got to gather information.

Morning arrived bringing with it all the physical imperatives of country living. Food and a drink first seemed to be the order of things. There was considerable activity below as his bedfellows all followed suit, Arthur joined a small bevy of attractive brown ladies sipping round a puddle in a rut. The fellow he had met in the garden last evening approached then, seeing who it was, waited patiently and pretended to be inspecting a clump of pale toadstools. The brown ladies nodded to each other and looked with more interest at Arthur's fine bronze chest and smart collar. Arthur pretended not to notice and continued drinking. The nearest feeder was round the walled garden and off down the drive, or he could try the feedstore and be a bit more careful about keeping watch. Everyone else seemed to reckon the feeder down the drive was the place to go to so he joined the trail round the walled garden. But once on the drive with the stable yard gate only thirty yards away it seemed foolish not to just have a look; besides it would be so much quicker and he'd be back round to the house that much sooner - and he was impatient. Three of the brown ladies were watching him and when he went purposefully towards the yard gate they exchanged glances. He was obviously going for food and it appeared that he knew about something, which they didn't but which they felt they ought to. They scuttled expectantly after him.

The foodstore door lay open but the bin was shut. Arthur peered about carefully as he slowly stepped in. The three hens were intrigued as they saw him go through the door but they were afraid to even enter the yard and paced about in indecision before the nerve of one broke and she ran off down the drive quickly followed by the other hen. Arthur meanwhile opened a bag of maize from the pile on the floor by pulling the little white string. Maize cascaded onto the ground and he started to fill his crop glancing round every few beakfulls. Once full he went quickly back out into the yard, drank from a puddle then flew up onto the roof ridge as he had done the morning before. Time only for a good look round, nobody about: the bathroom window was open again so he glided down to the lawn below it. More checking round, all OK. Right up we go, as quietly as possible this time. He perched on the open sill and listened for a full two minutes. There were sounds below but all was quiet upstairs, so Arthur felt emboldened. He hopped softly down onto the carpet and creeping over to the door tried to peep through the crack by the hinges but there was not much view of the room. 'Bother,'he thought but the silence continued so very very slowly he peered round the bathroom door. The room was empty - no Helen sitting watching this time. A few quick paces and he was at the bedroom door and ever so slowly he looked out onto the landing, still nothing; but sounds definitely coming up from the kitchen, not voices just sounds. Those indecipherable noises that accompany the brewing of tea, only easily recognized by fellow tea makers. The hollow little 'plonks' of the lid being replaced on the comfortably round earthenware jar that contains the tea bags, the clink of a teaspoon being placed on a saucer: the sound of the fridge door being opened in the quest for milk and behind all the little singing sounds of the kettle coming to the boil. By now Arthur was at the head of the stairs. Suddenly he heard a plug being pulled in the bathroom along the passage. The hall clock started to chime. "Now" - he nearly overbalanced, his tail went up his head went down, then off he pattered down the stairs across the hall and sprang up onto the top of the dresser near the front door. Heart pumping he crouched out of sight, but the clock was still methodically making its way through the routine. He had not been heard. Anne was coming down the stairs in her dressing gown and went into the kitchen before the clock had finished striking eight.

The top of the dresser was like a broad shelf with a moulded surround that was raised from the surface. The whole being well over six feet from the floor, this afforded excellent concealment for a crouching bird. It was pretty dusty and he shared his hiding place with a number of long forgotten items, which were draped in cobwebs. By wriggling to the end nearest the kitchen door he hoped to hear any conversation within. Hiding there in the dust on a shelf in his own home eavesdropping on his family in the hope of finding out where he was seemed so preposterous. He wanted to laugh, to shout aloud, even to cry but had to settle for a very vicious peck at a spider whose living space he had invaded.

"What time are you going in this morning?" It was Anne asking. They must be sitting either side of the kitchen table looking out over the lawn.

"I think in about an hour." Helen replied, "and then I'll go to Tesco's on the way home. Would you like to come?"

Any reply was drowned to Arthur by a door banging and various thumping noises, which accompanied George on his morning descent. George had an irritating habit of shutting doors as he moved about the house, doors that Arthur made a point of leaving open. An open door was an invitation to step through and meant whoever was in the room wanted others to know that there was always a welcome, The open door meant also that they were all at it together so to speak. Closed doors were like turned backs and seemed to be saying "I'm in here and I want privacy, go away, or knock." Arthur didn't think George did it consciously so he hadn't remonstrated, merely went about quietly opening the offending doors - sometimes he felt like taking them off their hinges but that would be thought a bit absurd. Maybe it was something to do with going to boarding school he mused. Must be that he concluded; draughty places inhabited by fairly rude young men and prowling prefects would be enough to make anyone cultivate the habit of shutting everything one could. Anyway since the kitchen door had now been firmly closed all he could hear were intermittent murmurings but he had a result. Tesco's Temple to Mammon was on the outskirts of a town with only one hospital about twelve miles away. He'd been to that hospital as a visitor and had a rough idea of the layout. It was a jumble of buildings ancient and modern that made a rabbit warren look well planned and it was right in the middle of the town. What a nuisance. Why couldn't it have been that nice private one, all ground floor, simply laid out, in the middle of the countryside surrounded by its own well planted grounds - and not so far away.

This was decision time. He felt sure that his only hope was to find himself face to face. He knew that. But, now that he knew what it all entailed, Arthur was afraid. He'd never seen a gamebird in the middle of town and for a very good reason, survival was a problem. But then again, Arthur had the brains and as the defense industry would say 'a flying capability'. Surely this combination would win him through.

Suddenly the kitchen door opened and Helen's head was no more than three feet from his beak, which opened and shut in silent exasperation She went off upstairs leaving Arthur to the sound of George munching his toast. Teal came padding out of the kitchen next, stopping suddenly at the foot of the stairs. Arthur couldn't see him for he had crouched well down when he heard the patter of feet but he could feel him standing with his head in the air questing with his nose. Teal whined, not a certain whine, but the querulous whine of possible excitement; he knew something but wasn't sure what it was. Mercifully this was interrupted by George coming out and saying "Well what's up with you then? Do you want out?"

Teal didn't want 'out' at all in particular but he wanted something so he wagged his tail in response which confirmed to George that he'd asked the right question.

"Come on then let's have a sniff around", he said batting Teal on the shoulder as he went across the hall and opened the front door.

They both went out. Through the window Arthur watched them walk off across the lawn going round to the right. He hopped down and ran to the front door; a quick check round then scuttled off to the left into the nearest flower bed and on down to a clump of shrubs.

As Anne came out of the kitchen cradling her second cup of tea she thought she saw something that looked like tail feathers disappearing through the front door. "Can't be" she thought, and frowning she turned and plodded up the stairs.

CHAPTER 3

Arthur hovered about in the shrubbery. Until now circumstances had rather carried him along but now he had to make an important decision about a potentially difficult and dangerous journey. He was hovering because he thought that if he could hop unseen into Helen's car much of the effort and danger would be by-passed. But maybe she was going in Anne's... or George's. Alternatively he could make the journey on foot. He knew the farms along the way quite well and could map out a relatively safe route and could even think of one or two places where the feeding might be quite good. There being no such thing as a packed lunch.

The question of the car was settled. George drove Helen's car round from the garage and was parking by the front door. It was an ubiquitous sort of estate car made in the Far East and having the advantage of four wheel drive. George sprang out and he and Teal disappeared into the house leaving the car door open! Considering all the door shutting that went on inside this was too much of an invitation - or a sign. Arthur moved from supine observation into top running speed, into the car, through between the seats and down under the passenger seat all in one headlong rush. The tail was a problem but if he moved so that it was stretching out along the floor towards the door he could sweep it under an empty shopping bag.

Two minutes later Helen got in. Then George's voice said, "Shall we take Teal?" No no! shouted Arthur inwardly? please no!

"Yes dear, I'm sure he'd like to come with us" was Helen's reply.

To his huge relief Teal was put in the back behind the 'dog guard'. Not a very robust affair when it is the only thing between one and a carnivorous animal several times one's own height, but quite sufficient though, to keep a dirty wet dog from casually jumping onto the back seats. Then Arthur's ceiling descended on him as George got in and he couldn't have made a hasty retreat even if he wanted to. They were hardly half way down the drive before Teal whined and by the time they reached the Lodge gate George turned and told him to "Lie down", which Teal, being a well trained fellow, did. His nose did not stop telling him about the pheasant somewhere in the car though and he was consumed with curiosity.

Apart from the odd comment about their surroundings, Helen and George did not talk much during the journey and with a short "well, here we are then", the car stopped and they both got out. 'Wait wait' but there was no time for Arthur to get out too, he had been a bit flattened and wasn't quick off the mark. The doors were locked and he was alone in the car with Teal who knew he was there and who was not going to let this knowledge be unused:

Teal stood up with ears cocked forward and tail out behind, quivering a little. Arthur had eased himself out from under the seat and was crouched flattened on the floor just out of sight. The front driver's window was open a crack, not a big enough crack for a pheasant, Arthur lay very still. There was a little whine from the back followed by an excited woof, Arthur's wings trembled but he never stirred.

More whining followed, then Teal dabbed at the dog guard with a front paw, and snuffled at the waft of scent that rose from so near. Then suddenly he barked with impotent excitement. Arthur practically fell out of his feathers with shock at the noise and he jumped through onto the front seat. But he'd been seen for an instant, Teal knew exactly who had been creating the scent and precisely where that person was. Sitting on the front seat! In the car! A cock pheasant for him to retrieve, this should never be. So he 'marked and scrabbled at the flimsy bars.

"Oh God help me, this is awful" thought Arthur and cried aloud his most alarming alarm call; he couldn't help it. Far from shutting Teal up he drove him to more noise and pawing. It wasn't right: there shouldn't be a bird in the car, something was wrong. The scent was a pheasant but everything else was wrong, Teal didn't understand and it made him angry so he shouted aloud.

Helen and George had just arrived in the private room overlooking the car park from the second floor, where 'Arthur' was now lying. In a stable coma as far as the specialist could understand these things and so not in need of all the paraphernalia of intensive care. Hardly had they taken in the peaceful scene in the room when they both became aware of the barking below and recognized what it might be. George went straight over to the window and looked down,

"It is Teal. What on earth is happening?"

"Go and find out, darling", Helen said then looked down at 'Arthur' wondering if he too might recognize the barking.

Arthur could in fact hardly stand the barking any more. He was praying that the bars of the dog guard would hold. Now and again Teal stopped barking and wrestled with the bars in his teeth, there seemed to be some give in them so he braced himself tugging at them. Arthur sprung into view calling loudly in an effort to make Teal let go. Better to be deafened by noise than to be grabbed by teeth.

George was running across the car park. Oh quicker please! With amazement at what he saw through the window, Teal fell over with a crash in the back as the dog guard gave way to his pulling, George opened the door fumbling with the key shouting at him to sit down and Arthur threw himself out of the opening, slipped, fell, scrabbled off round the next car and took off to land in a sycamore tree at the other end of the car park. Where he let off a whole series of staccato alarm calls to recover from his fright. Passers by stopped and stared at this unusual sight, two nurses in blue cloaks pointed and laughed. Helen had seen it all from the window but as the pheasant's alarm call echoed round outside the hospital she turned to Arthur's bedside, sure that he had groaned and stirred. Quickly she rang for the nurse.

George grabbed hold of Teal as he clambered over the seats and holding him by the collar calmed him down telling him what a good boy he had been and how extraordinary it was and wondering how on earth that pheasant had got into the car. Then putting Teal on his lead he walked down to the sycamore tree and looked up.

Arthur found himself in an embarrassing and ludicrous situation without the faintest idea what to do next. He looked down at his son and his dog with a beady eye. George stared at him.

"You're the same bird from the bathroom aren't you?"

"Yes yes"Arthur seemed to say, instead he hopped down a few branches to be closer, and cocked his head to one side trying to mime friendship, fatherhood being too far altogether.

"What on earth are you up to?" George asked.

Arthur made a cooing noise, it was the best he could do, communication was impossible but he must make some contact. Then Helen was calling George from the main door of the hospital.

"I'll see you again Mr Pheasant" he said and turned and went. Arthur was emotionally drained, but Helen was flushed and excited.

"He moved and made a noise" she cried taking George by the arm and they hurried back up to the room after putting Teal back in the car. The screen was blipping quietly, a doctor was testing reflexes, looking for reactions but he could find no indication that there had been any activity conscious or unconscious. He smiled a reassuring non-committal smile as they came in.

"Well?" asked Helen somewhat expectantly.

"I'm delighted you saw a movement, but I can't detect any change in his condition at the moment. All his reflexes are as they were but that isn't to say something has not or will not happen."

"Maybe it was the sound of Teal that got through to him," said George seeing his mother begin to look combative.

"That is perfectly possible" the doctor replied a little bit tongue tied with the knowledge that relatives will read much into nothing or even dare one think it, imagine things that have not happened. He continued probing the patient, listening with his stethoscope as a means of avoiding more conversation. A nurse returned and took on the burden of talking to the relatives.

In the sycamore tree Arthur was trying to regain his composure. He was rather noticeable. George's place below had been taken by an ugly youth pushing an old man in a wheel chair, they both stared up at him and told him what a pretty boy he was. If it wasn't for the fact that his mind was rather preoccupied this would be quite insufferable. Then the ugly youth threw a pebble at him with the words "Go on, move yer bugger!" The stone bounced among the branches.

"What you do that fer?" asked the old man querulously.

"Well its only a silly bird sitting doing nothing", came the staggering reply, and he bent to pick up another stone. Arthur did not wait but launched into flight landing in part of the hospital garden beyond the car park then he hopped up into the lower branches of a cedar tree.

There were quite a lot of birds in the garden and they all seemed to tolerate his intrusion except a wren who appeared to be saying things just as rude as the repulsive youth, but who could be ignored through her inability to throw stones. The very fat wood pigeons were making their way across one of the lawns, and a blackbird was having success on another. Somewhere round the corner of the physiotherapy unit a thrush was murdering a snail with loud and squashy taps and from the rose bed in front came the aggressive song of a self important little robin warning other self important little cock robins to make themselves scarce. At least here he was not the centre of human attention and from here he could observe quite a few of the windows. Arthur had not seen Helen looking out so he had no idea which room or ward to be looking for. Correction it must be one where they could hear a dog barking in the car park, so he would concentrate on the windows facing that way, there were three floors of them with about sixteen to a floor!

By midday he was fairly satisfied that neither of the bottom two floors required any further investigation and had made his way to the higher branches of the cedar to eye the top floor. This was much harder as the windows appeared to belong to separate rooms, rather than the wards of lower down and he could not look down into the rooms being able only to perch at the same level. In the time Arthur had been watching he hadn't noticed George look out of the window twice, since his eyes had been concentrating elsewhere. But he did see George and Helen come out of the hospital and walk towards the car. They looked around but didn't see him way up in the cedar branches, they got in and drove out of the car park. Now what? Arthur was beginning to feel a bit forlorn and rather tired. The odd pang of hunger was creeping up on him.

On the terrace in the garden below was a large bird table overlooked by the French window of the women's geriatric ward on the ground floor. The nurses put out food for the birds in the morning and later in the afternoon, much to the pleasure of their patients. Arthur had seen the table but at present there was nothing on it. He was rather keeping it in mind. His immediate problem was to see inside each room opposite and to do so there was the same difficulty as he had experienced when trying to enter the bathroom of his own home. His flying ability dictated that to go from one window sill to another meant that each one would have to be approached separately with vertical take off from below though it might be worth a try to fly from one to another.

'Right' he thought, time to make a start. A thorough survey of activity in the car park showed a medical figure approaching the front door and two people walking away at the far end. As soon as the medical person was gone Arthur set his wings and drifted down to a very neat landing in a reserved parking space to the right of the main door. Another glance around and up he went with all concentration on the sill above. The landing was very difficult and he nearly panicked, with wings working his feet slipped and slithered on the smooth narrow concrete sill, he pressed his chest against the window and kept flapping away to gain some balance. It took a full minute of supreme effort to become steady and secure enough to stop flapping and crouch motionless on the ledge. Arthur felt extremely unsafe. The slightest movement and he felt his feet losing purchase. His tail hung over the edge and his chest was hard up against the window pane. He looked in. The room was empty.

The thought of doing this sixteen times was overwhelming. Just the once had been a huge effort. He would try to land on the next sill without going down and up again. As far as he could see there was still no one about and his performance had not been noticed. A few more deep breaths and he hopped off into the air. Wings beating frantically, he was on the next sill in a second, landing too fast with a bump against the glass. Staring in with a sort of horror he saw his self, lost balance, banged one wing hard against the brickwork and toppled over. Out of control, Arthur flapped furiously and painfully, fighting gravity without success he hurtled along the side of the hospital in a blur of feathers, almost regained some balance by kicking at the walls whizzing past, tried to set his wings out for a glide and an attempt at landing and fetched up hard against the bird table.

Inside the ordered severity of the hospital two things happened. One was the sounding of the emergency warning bleeper in the staff nurses' office for one of the private rooms. The nurse fled along the corridor to find Mr Beamish, their patient in a coma, had fallen out of bed!

"How on earth.... " said one

"Never mind ... emergency bell...quick!" and the other thumping the patient on the chest to rouse the absent pulse. Other white coated figures flighted in like a covey of partridges - armed with an emergency trolley they worked swiftly to resuscitate the patient, and soon all the bits and pieces of intensive care were amassed around the bed.

Simultaneously in the geriatric ward downstairs there were squalls of concern from several elderly sufferers who were sitting looking out through the tall windows. They were amazed to witness a large cock pheasant come hurtling round the side of the hospital and dash itself against the bird table. As it lay on the terrace amidst a quantity of loose feathers a nurse hurried down the ward to see what the trouble was. A porter was summoned to remove the seemingly dead bird.

It happened that the porter on duty, a kindly grey haired man in his final year before retirement, was delighted by the request to remove the bird. He was a great one for pets and wild creatures, having a loft of pigeons and an aviary of small birds in his cottage garden. So to deal with this request tickled his interest. He bent down and put his hand under Arthur's wing, there was a steady pulse.

"He's only just knocked out," he told the watching audience

"No sign of damage...", he added gently handling Arthur's inert body.

"Isn't he a beauty?" The porter said showing the old ladies the lovely colour of Arthur's feathers. They were all pleased and delighted that he was still alive and looked so lovely and hoped the porter would find a nice place for it to recover in and go free. He said he certainly would and carried the unconscious bird away.

In the porter's rest room near the front door Mr O'Donaghue, for that was the porter's name, found himself a cardboard box, and having filled it with newspaper he laid his prize in it. Then he cellotaped the lid secure and punctured a few holes along one side. Satisfied that should the pheasant recover consciousness before the end of his shift it could not escape he patted the box with pleasure and went about his business.

Arthur remained prone, being in the darkness breathing steadily. Nor did he wake up when the box was lifted and carried out. O'Donaghue was a man who was proud of his possessions. He took a lot of care of these things and enjoyed doing so, one such pride and joy was his three wheeler car and it was into the back of this that he placed the cardboard box and set off for home. Maybe it was the uncomfortable motion of lolling about on the floor or the latent fear engendered by his last trip in a car that woke Arthur up. Either way his eyes suddenly opened and he began to wonder what on earth was going on. He lay there quite a while trying to figure out who and where he was. But memory plays tricks when you've had a sudden blow and he found himself in a state of confusion and having scrabbled onto his feet he just crouched there waiting for whatever was in store. The car stopped ... There was a creaking of doors and he felt himself being carried - more openings and shuttings and suddenly the box opened and light flooded in. A big face peered down at him and before Arthur knew what to do next large hands had lifted him firmly out.

The face was a kindly one. Arthur found himself feeling reassured by the O'Donaghue voice, soothingly telling him what a beautiful big boy he was and to what a pleasant and comfortable place he had been brought. This was all very well but what on earth had been happening in the meanwhile - where was he? The O'Donaghue voice droned on. Arthur had never been held in quite such close proximity to another man in all his life and it made him feel really rather uncomfortable when the O'Donoghue lips brushed along the top of his head he would have come out in a cold sweat had he been able - Instead he had an uncontrollable urge to peck at the object of his fear and did so quite violently. Fiercely enough to draw blood from the squashy part of Mr O'Donaghue's lower lip.

"Oh you wicked brute!" cried the porter, more startled than angry. His birds often reacted to initial handling with a few pecks. Pigeons were not so strong as pheasants and he could usually disregard them until they tired of doing it. With this fellow though, he thought one peck was enough for the time being so he opened the door of a wire netting pen at the back of the shed they were in and popped Arthur down on the sawdust floor. Then he fetched a bowl of mixed corn with a few maple peas as well and put that through the door in front of Arthur.

Arthur just stood watching. Above him on a perch were two turtle doves. There were other empty perches and a water drinker in the corner on the floor and now a big bowl of food right under his nose. The kindly face above him did not appear to be cross about the peck and Arthur now felt rather sorry for what he had done. He wished to make amends. To say sorry and thank you for the food and above all ask his captor where he was and what was going to happen. Mr O'Donaghue obligingly started to tell him.

"Well my fine fellow" he was saying "If you eat up your food and look like you're all right we must think of where to let you out back to the woods where you'll be safe. I'll put you in a pen in the garden tomorrow and see how you shape up." He stood looking at Arthur for a while then set about tending to his other creatures before going into the cottage and tending to himself. There had never been a Mrs O'Donaghue, which went some way to explaining his delight in having a collection of birds.

Now that he was alone Arthur tucked in to the dish of assorted grain in front of him, rather relishing the peas which he had never eaten in this state before. Once having filled his crop he started to look around. The turtle doves didn't know what to make of him as they kept bowing and bobbing looking at him first with one bright eye then the other. He certainly didn't feel terribly interested in them. Getting out was what was important. The wire netting door had a clasp with a peg in it on the outside. Not much hope there. The rest of the netting seemed neatly and regularly stapled all the way round even up at the apex of the roof - pity, not even a loose one. But wait, up on a level with the perches was a shelf and what looked like a pop hole. Arthur wanted to say 'look out

I'm coming up' but couldn't so didn't. He just launched up to a perch causing the turtle doves complete consternation. They thought they were being attacked and crashed about in a frenzy, which only ceased when they lay puffing and battered on the floor.

Arthur was definitely becoming hardened and more cynical as a result of his curious position and merely passed the comment that they were stupid birds. Then seeing the irony of his words found himself wracked with uncontrollable mirth. It is hard for a pheasant to laugh not being equipped with a smile or a wagging tail, Arthur contented himself with a shaking of the shoulder and some odd little noises in the throat. Then suddenly feeling lonely he turned to the pop hole. There was room with a bit of waggling to ease his beak under and lever it up a fraction, then it jammed. With a bit more contortion he found he could shove one of his toes into the gap and let go with his beak so that the pop hole went loose again. Now another go with the beak and up it went. A quick flip with head and neck and he was looking up at the stars, his head outside but his body inside. The pop hole was designed for pigeons; pheasants were several sizes too large.

For a long time Arthur just sat there looking around wishing the hole to become larger. Even without feathers he knew he couldn't fit and Arthur felt aware that pheasants were as fond of their feathers as men were fond of their hair. Neither wished to be without if at all possible.

The night air was cool and clear, the stars were bright and each noise he heard told a tale. Occasional cars on a nearby road chasing to catch up the great funnel of light that preceded them, some hurrying some on the prowl; always a barking dog somewhere, not a happy sound. A little owl away across some meadow nearby, a helicopter winking light. A human cough, the sound of which can seemingly travel a great distance. All these sounds made Arthur part of the world and yet he wasn't. Melancholy was creeping up again and must be resisted. He withdrew himself into the shed and with heavy movements settled to sleep on one of the perches. An hour later the porter looked quietly into the shed, saw all was well and turned off the light letting the night settle in.

CHAPTER 4

Mary accompanied Helen to the hospital that evening, George had gone out with Emma and a party of friends and Anne said she would come the next morning. Arthur was back in his room but now his bed had little railings down both sides. A nurse was soon there to explain why and to point out that although there had been an emergency, there was now no detectable change in Arthur's condition from that morning. Indeed it was strange, not to say unique, that a man in a coma should fall out of bed or at least be found on the floor with a cardiac arrest. However cardiac arrest was a regular, though not numerically high, event in the hospital and no one took exception to it. No pressing questions from Helen could shake the nurse from her gentle acceptance of these traumatic events as any more than what was to be expected. In a way this was re-assuring for Helen and Mary but in another way made them fearful of 'normality'.

By way of changing the conversation the nurse recounted the tale of the pheasant knowing them to be country people. But far from disturbing Helen this seemed to unexpectedly raise her to excitement. Something clicked within. This was one coincidence too many. Why were they being plagued by this pheasant ever since Arthur's collapse.

"There must be a connection" Helen declared almost shouting. Mary was worried "How can there be?" she queried.

"Do you think its following Daddy for something. A vendetta for being shot at".

"I don't know, I don't understand. But there's something happening. It's the same bird, I'm sure, or the one that crowed at us in the field just after Daddy's heart attack. It had a large white ring round its neck and every time I see this bird it also has a large white ring." Helen turned to the nurse who was looking rather apprehensive

"Did the bird this afternoon have a pronounced white ring?"

"I don't know" she replied, "but I can ask the porter, I believe he took it home with him."

"Where is he now?" asked Helen, the bit firmly between her teeth.

"He went home this evening I think. He'll be back in the morning .

"What's his name and his address?"

"Oh I don't know I think you had better ask the administrator; we call him Matthew."

"Thank you, now where do I find the administrator?" persisted Helen quietly now but firmly.

"Down on the ground floor next door to reception, but there may be no one there at this time" replied the nurse "Everyone will certainly be here in the morning."

Helen and Mary went back to Arthur's bedside.

"I know there's a connection" Helen said with conviction. "Why should it come into the house, then come with us in the car. And why should Arthur fall out of bed while this bird is crashing around outside?" Mary was at a loss to know what answer to give and wondered too why or how her unconscious father lying there peacefully before them could possibly fall out of the bed.

Helen went down to find the administrator but to no avail and no one seemed to know the porter's address or if they did they felt obliged not to give it out but deferred instead to higher authority. She returned and sat beside Mary, pondering. When they left an hour later there had been no change in Arthur's state, no sign or hint of anything to help their minds journey down this unknown path.

****

Arthur awoke the next morning at dawn as he normally did now. It was funny how easy it was to wake up now that he had assumed the habit of a bird. Other creatures appeared to have no problem with not wanting to get up. Birds come awake as the grey light spreads, refreshed and interested in the days foraging to come with the minimum of yawning and stretching. It is only man who has moved his waking time so that it no longer coincides with daylight. The dairyman and the lambing shepherd know full well the wasted hours of other members of their species, but maybe that is why they appreciate witnessing the fresh dawning time the more - it is theirs alone, unsullied by others; they feel privileged to be closer to the ways of nature on their own. As for the birds it is more like the rush hour.

The turtle doves had got over their fear of this monstrous brute who shared their home as long as the monstrous brute was static. Arthur eyed them as they cooed and preened and dropped down for a drink.

'Mmm, very industrious' he thought.

The main thought that had crystallized in his mind overnight was one of escape. Whatever the porter had said didn't necessarily mean that he would be set free. But escape to do what, he wasn't yet sure. The thought of returning to the hospital was rather fearsome. He would rather go home, but was that him just feeling like a ninny or was it the best thing to do? Either way he couldn't do anything as long as he was a prisoner. He sorted out a few feathers that seemed in need of immediate grooming before dropping down for a drink, to the renewed alarm of the turtle doves, who found movement of the monster rather worrying. There was still some mixed corn in the dish so he polished it off listening the while for his captor's approach.

This was not long in coming. Matthew O'Donoghue had a number of things to do before going off to work and feeding his birds took a little while, because he liked to have a good look at them in the morning and pass a word or two with each. He was talking quite loudly to his pigeon loft as he opened the shed door; then in a more gentle tone he wished Arthur and the doves good morning while he filled a bucket with grain. This he took off outside, leaving the door open. There were chickens, pigeons and ducks to be fed and let out. It all took quite a time, and the voice chattered on round the garden opening pop holes, filling water drinkers. Arthur felt twitchy as he stood resolutely by the feed bowl facing the netting door of his pen. The porter was returning preceded by his voice. He fiddled about by his feed bags then turned to the pen door with a hand bowl.

"How are you then, feeling better. My word but you're a beauty? Here's some breakfast for you then." The door was opened and the porter bent towards Arthur to fill the dish from his handbowl. From pretending to be utterly still and relaxed Arthur scuttled forward round his legs and before he could react at all, Arthur had bounced through the door and ran out of the shed. Free outside he paused looking fiercely round 'where to now?' He ran a few paces over the grass towards a chicken ark and stopped again.

Matthew O'Donaghue was standing in the door way smiling and watching "You're all right now then lovely boy" he said. Arthur suddenly felt considerable friendship for this man. Now he was free, they could be equals, there was no need to fly off into the middle distance. So he puffed out his feathers a bit and relaxed and nodded assent at this 'being all right now.' The porter threw a few handfulls of grain onto the grass, then remembering that he had a job to go to finished up in the shed and went back into his cottage. A few minutes later he came out again and was pleased to see Arthur helping himself to the scattered grain. He waved and drove off.

Two hours later while busily manoeuvering a trolley load of linen across the hall a nice looking grey haired lady approached him.

"Matthew O'Donaghue?" she asked.

"That's me "he replied.

"I wonder if l could ask you about a pheasant?" the lady continued and proceeded to recount to him what she regarded as the saga of the ring necked cock. Matthew listened fascinated and when she had finished said "You must go and look for him directly" and he told her part of the tale and how the bird had eluded him but also how it had not rushed wildly off.

"l think it must be in the way of being tame. But more than that, I could not disagree with what you say. l do not know enough of things to guess at what the fellow is up to. You go and find him." And he gave Helen directions as to how to find his cottage and whereabouts in the garden that he had last seen Arthur. A little while after she had gone, during what ostensibly was his coffee break; the porter slipped up to the private room where the patient Arthur Beamish lay. He looked at him closely and for several minutes, then out of the window, watching and wondering. He enjoyed a conundrum.

Less than half an hour had elapsed before Helen drew up in the lane outside the porter's cottage. She opened the little latch gate and walked up the path looking round, searching for a glimpse of burnished feathers. The front garden was neat and unencumbered with avian activity, but when she penetrated round behind as instructed she found the back premises more resembled a free range poultry yard. There were ducks under the shrubs and bantams in the apple trees, pigeons marching about on every available shed roof. Nobody took a great deal of notice of her, bright eyes were cocked in her direction but when their owners decided there were no food parcels involved they went back to their own business of preening, squabbling or just resting. Nowhere was there any sign of any pheasant. She searched thoroughly causing a bit of disturbance in her diligence; she opened the shed where Arthur had spent the night. She looked out over the surrounding fields then left the garden and walked out beyond its boundaries. As she stood looking down a wide hedgerow that led off towards a clump of trees the urge to call "Where are you. What do you want?" rose strongly in her throat. Helen contained the words feeling embarrassed at herself, then tearful. And then again, cross with her weakness she did call out. There was no one about, why should she be shy in front of a collection of birds. She called again louder, more demanding. Who was going soft in the head? Reason had nothing to do with this feeling. A feeling that something had to be put right. A settling of souls. Something had to be retrieved.

But it couldn't be done without finding the pheasant. For two hours she walked in wider circles round the cottage, encompassing the fields, two small copses, a small overgrown stream, the lane in its deep hedgerows. Beyond one of the copses she disturbed three hen pheasants and on seeing them legging away up the stubble rows Helen gave chase shouting at them to stop. This put the fear of God into them and they put up their tails and ran like stink.

Her activities had not gone unnoticed and as she ran up the stubble field a landrover stolidly approached from the other side of the field. Helen became aware of it and stopped. She was distraught, it was obvious she had been crying, her hair was all blown about and she certainly wasn't dressed for a country walk. A lined and weathered face looked out of the landrover, it spoke.

"Can I help you, Madam?" then becoming more aware that all was not well and help really was needed the owner of the face switched off his machine and getting out asked in a gentler tone.

"Are you all right?"

By now Helen was more organized.

“I was looking for a pheasant” she said getting rather hot in the cheeks, “It was in the garden this morning but has gone”.

The owner of the face thought about that for a moment then replied more in the tone of the prep school master who has found a small boy outside the fruit cupboard

“And which garden might that be?”

“The one down there” said Helen pointing in the direction of the cottage which was now obscured by the copse and a good half mile off. The moment had gone when she could have spilled herself out, instead, she apologized for being where she was, explained that the bird in question had spent the night in one of the sheds and accepted the offer of a lift back to the cottage. With no more explanation forthcoming conversation was rather short and stilted and there were no offers of help in the search. The normal world seemed to have closed in. Helen thanked her escort rather distantly, returned to her car and drove home in confusion.

****

Three miles away Arthur was standing in the tussocky grass of the wide roadside verge reading a signpost as the traffic thundered past. He was where he thought he was going to be when he had set off from the cottage garden but then he had not been sure. He was some eight miles the other side of town, from home. Eight miles to the hospital, twenty miles home.

After bidding Matthew O’Donoghue goodbye, Arthur had joined the other inhabitants of the O’Donoghue menage for the rest of his breakfast. Then he had flown up onto the cottage roof to survey the scene and try to work out where he was. The countryside to the south was indeterminate and not a lot was visible, but to the north large arable fields sloped upwards in an undulating wave and the distant pine trees on the far horizon could be by the road that he had now confirmed he knew. Walking up the arable fields had been a doddle. Firm dry open ground with little remnants of hedges sketched in long straight lines was not the sort of country to harbour dangers, or much life at all for that matter. The distant brown lump of a crouching hare was the only other living thing he had encountered. But here by the roadside a positive stream of human life was pouring by in both directions.

This was a time of choice. Though after a little consideration it seemed to Arthur that there was only one choice and that was to somehow return to the hospital and try more carefully to confront his other self. There really didn't seem to be an alternative. He couldn't just return home and live in the walled garden watching the house and awaiting the return of this other self from hospital. How long would that be? What was the ailment? Whereas he knew he could do something now because he knew exactly where to find himself, the only difficulty was logistical. 'Fine' he thought 'eight miles is no distance. I'll fly north and approach through the town school's playing fields". From there it was not a long flight on a down gradient to the hospital grounds.

Arthur knew roughly the layout of the countryside between himself and his destination, undulating hills of mixed arable and pasture with quite a lot of woodland dotted about. The road he stood by led to some distant town to the south, his direct route lay across country on the other side.

All the time he had been standing there in view of the road there had not appeared a single opportunity to cross it without fear of being squashed by some speeding juggernaut. Arthur waited and watched for a few minutes, then seeing a possible gap approaching he moved nearer to the roadside unaware of the passing motorists stares. The gap came and with a quick dash he was over the first hurdle through the hedge and off across an empty grass field.

For two hours he plodded on. It was a clear breezy day, with clouds running across the sky but mostly plenty of sunshine. Out of the wind on the sunny side of hedges it was positively warm and this was where he met most activity. By keeping to the open where possible he only met rooks, pigeons and seagulls and occasionally a group of partridges.

But each field had a border and he approached the hedges with caution. Quite often there appeared to be a resident cock pheasant usually on the sunny side and he gave them a reasonably wide birth since he was in no mood to waste energy in an argument. In two hours he never saw a person just a tractor two fields away taking a bale of silage to some cattle and the only danger had been a far distant fox that never gave him a second glance. But now he had come over a brow and was looking out across some countryside that looked more complicated. Houses and farms were dotted all along the valley and small woods ran in ribbons round them: the fields were smaller and the hedges thicker, larger arable fields lay on the slopes beyond, well over a mile away.

Arthur was not an experienced flier, on top of that he felt somewhat stiff and bruised from his encounter with the bird table, A mornings steady walking had left him feeling rather tired and hungry. On the other hand the most sensible course of action would be to fly right across this area of possible dangers, he was up on a hill and with all the advantages of height he ought to get a long way without great effort. He hesitated out of ignorance.

Way up in the sunlight to his left a buzzard was soaring effortlessly drifting on the wind; out in the vale rooks were moving about calling to each other as they flew easily about their business; the wood pigeons hurried by side slipping across the breeze to alter course.

"Smug blighters" thought Arthur fighting with his nerves. However, he had seen enough pheasants sailing out across enough valleys, all one needed was to gain height then set the wings and glide with the occasional flap to extend ones trajectory. There was another slight worry and that was the occasional rattle of gunfire that he had been hearing now and then all morning. Normally this would have given him a pleasing feel of anticipation now it sent small shivers through his being. He was most anxious not to get involved in these sporting activities!

As is often the case when the indecisive dawdle, events overtake them and decisions are forced up on them. So it was in Arthur's case, his reverie of thought and consideration was burst in upon by the sudden arrival of two galloping Irish setters that came hurtling over the hill behind him. Tongues flapping, great mouthfuls of teeth and gasping breath sent him straight up into orbit. The rush of adrenalin lent energy to his wings as he towered up into the sky. Fear was abandoned in the pleasure of his performance, he exulted in his strength, further and higher! This was marvellous, what a feeling!

The lady on horseback trailing in the wake of the setters, on seeing Arthur's flight called to her distant dogs and told them what clever boys they were, not that they heard or cared for they too were exulting in their own energy as they careered on down the slope.

A few seconds of this tremendous feeling of power were all that Arthur could maintain so he levelled out to glide and work his wings more sparingly. By now he was out across the valley well over three hundred feet above the houses and farmsteads, going smoothly faster, than he had supposed but with a lot of woodland yet to cross. The wind rushed by and he found he had to concentrate quite hard on looking ahead and maintaining a course. He was working hard but all the time loosing height. This was some work, he didn't have enough energy now to gain height. A landing had to be made soon, he couldn't clear the next wood coming up. The landing Arthur made at the edge of the wood was not very elegant but at least he remained upright. He gathered himself together shaking his feathers into order and folding his wings in a more orderly fashion. Arthur stood looking round taking deep breaths and relaxing his trembling wing muscles. 'Golly what a performance. What a terrific feeling!' he thought.

The edge of the wood was open with only an electric fence to contain any livestock in the field and looking in through the stems of hazel and boles of oak and ash Arthur could see plenty of varied cover and well used paths leading away further in. Along the edge another cock pheasant was eyeing him suspiciously as were a number of other cocks and hens beyond him. They did not appear worried or aggressive but they were wondering what had made him fly. Their presence spelt food and keepering and their demeanor spelt peace, so Arthur picked his way slowly towards them in the hope of locating some sustenance. He drank lengthily from some water in a hoof print and by the time he was near them none of them seemed too bothered by his intrusion. The first cock looked rather big and important so Arthur circled round showing deference, he felt far too whacked to pick a fight and moving on along the edge of the group he saw an area of loose straw leading into a ride and what looked like a feed hopper deeper within the trees.

'What luck' he mused, 'a transport café just where its needed.' Passing by a number of other birds, some of whom nodded a greeting, he approached the hopper then stood a bit nonplussed. Obviously by the bare ground under it grain was dispensed to those who wanted it, but how? There was no mesh underneath for grain to fall through, no hatch to poke your head in, no slits up the side; just a yellow knob of plastic on the end of a wire protruding from the bottom.

There were definitely times when it was exasperating not to have the power of speech. All these plump contented birds in the vicinity obviously knew exactly how to extract food from this contraption. In his boyhood Arthur had fondly believed that birds and animals could converse with each other albeit in a rather simple fashion. After all he had been taught that mere bees could tell each other exactly where a distant heather bank was located and that migrating geese organized themselves in squadrons for the journey. Why then should not ducks make themselves understood to each other or robins in the garden; but as he grew he came to realize that this could not be so. If it was why did the cows stay in the field? Why did not every bird in the country visit the feed store when the feed bin was open so much? Now the reason why man was so very much in charge of things was being pressed home.

The yellow plastic thing must be the key: he gave it a tentative peck which caused a cascade of wheat to fall out of somewhere. How simple. So between pecking the plastic and gathering the scattered results Arthur filled his crop in quite a short time. Such was his feeling of well being that he felt he could indulge in a short rest in the sunshine amongst his fellows.

The peace did not last long. The first intimation of impending chaos was the banging of car doors some long way off at the far end of the wood. Arthur heard it and opened an eye, other birds had cocked their heads and were listening. A jay sounded its warning and came flying slowly towards them switchbacking through the trees. Everyone was alert by now, even more so when the sound of a human cough travelled up from the other end of the wood. A hen pheasant came hurrying up the side of the trees towards them, disturbed by whoever had been shutting car doors. But she stopped and they all jumped a bit when they heard a shout of laughter from the direction of the cough. A figure appeared in the field, he was smiling from the amusement of a good joke and he was carrying a gun.

Arthur felt agitated, the others were agitated, it was catching. They all moved into the wood to take cover.

'Calm down and think' commanded Arthur to his anxious feet. A horn sounded and immediately noises began down at the end of the wood where the man with a gun was visible. So the answer was simple, the beater had walking guns and the standing guns were near the car doors all he had to do was scuttle off across the field and crouch by one of the large oak trees dotted about out there on their own or better still hop up into the branches and stay there until the drive was over and the shooting party had moved on. This Arthur did straight away, and from his seat on a branch pressed up against the main trunk for concealment he had a grandstand view.

There was much whistling and tapping as the line moved up the wood and the birds amongst the trees moved on well ahead of the noise towards the other end. A few clapped down where they felt they had such effective hiding places that no one could possibly find them and some were right, others were not so lucky. A bustling spaniel can penetrate the thickest of bramble patches and even if it might not actually find a hiding bird the tremendous noise it makes with plunging in will often unnerve the crouching pheasant into forsaking its hiding place; then there is danger indeed. The first bird to explode from such a retreat was either lucky or wise since it took off back over the beaters and flew away unsaluted. The second one was not so bright and flew out sideways right into the arc of fire of the walking figure with a gun. He did not miss. The bird fell hard onto the turf only forty yards from Arthur's tree and a voice startlingly close called out

"Well done Jim, I'll pick it up."

Crouched against the trunk, Arthur had not noticed the approach on the other side of another figure with a gun walking further out and slightly ahead of the first figure "Jim", The feathers tingled down his neck.

"Ah there you are my beauty", came a leary voice from below and Arthur looking down over his shoulder found himself faced with the wrong end of a double barrel shotgun.

"Hey Jim, there's a cock up here all right!"

"Well knock him out of there" Jim called back.

Arthur sat tight 'he wouldn't, he really wouldn't, would he?' The man below was sorely tempted to shoot the sitting bird, sportsmanlike considerations were not high on his agenda, he refrained only because of the presence of others. So threw a piece of dead branch up at Arthur to dislodge him and the spaniel at his heel then realized what was afoot. The branch nearly found its mark bouncing against the trunk just above Arthur's shoulder and as he wobbled and clung on a sod of turf took him fairly in the backside and he lost his balance with the shock.

'l must not fly',

'l must not fly', Arthur shouted within as he flopped and scrabbled down the side of the tree, bounced onto the ground and ran like fury.

'I must not fly' he chanted, legs going like pistons. The spaniel was after him closing fast, his crop was full.

'I must not fly', he couldn't go any faster. The man was swinging his gun. The spaniel was above him, he opened his wings and drove himself forward. Fifty yards, sixty, he was in the air the spaniel was falling behind - bang - ouch - great pain in his right wing he was down running again.

'I must not fly'. He ran fit to burst. The spaniel was fading. He was through the hedge forty yards ahead up and over the bank practically trod on a rabbit, who cares, keep running. The spaniel eased as the rabbit popped out where the pheasant had run in, it took off after it nearly succeeding in the surprise. By now Arthur was a hundred yards up the hedge in the opposite direction still going but not strong. In fact failing fast and feeling a bit dizzy. He went into the cover of the hedge and stopped, beak open and chest heaving.

'How bloody unsporting' was his first furious reaction 'No one should do that sort of thing'. He was gasping and speechless. The noise of the beaters had faded right away to be replaced by the sound of gun fire. At least he was safe but so sore. His wing seemed to be on fire particularly at the tip but also on the fore arm. Even trying to move it so that he could see the damage hurt abominably. He could half open it before it was too painful; he was bleeding and there was nothing he could do about it. He could just reach it with his beak but even that was sore and then what. By tucking up his wing in a state of repose the pain was eased a bit, so he did that and sat in the hedge keeping a lookout and feeling hurt and reflecting on how quickly things went from good to bad.

CHAPTER 5

At just after two o'clock the consultant left Arthur Beamish's room having viewed his patient closely. Everything appeared static and he went off slowly down the corridor discussing things with Sister. They left the young nurse on duty to change the drip and clear up. She adjusted the new drip, composed the patient's limbs put back up the cot-sides and turned to leave the room. She was just opening the door when there was a loud crash behind her. Startled she turned and saw to her horror what had happened. The drip stand had fallen over, the bedside cot-sides had dropped and the patient's arm was awry and bleeding where the needle had been wrenched out. Her shriek of surprise brought the consultant and Sister running back into the room. Things were even worse It seemed that two of the patient's fingers were broken having caught between the bars of the cot-side and the falling drip stand or so they thought.

"How can this possibly have happened?" demanded the consultant. Drip stands were extremely stable and could only fall if pulled quite violently.

"I didn't see, I was just opening the door. I had just secured the cot-sides after setting the drip, picked up the tray and was just coming out, when it just crashed."

"Are you sure you fastened the sides?" asked sister ominously frowning.

"Absolutely; and his arm was lying along like this", she had lifted Arthur's arm back and swabbed the torn needle hole. He must have moved."

"Nonsense" said the consultant, not altogether convincingly.

"Well he fell out of bed yesterday", the Sister agreed.

The consultant stroked his upper lip with his forefinger looking at them both from under his brows. Then gave Arthur's prone figure another thorough examination. There was no sign of recent activity.

His fingers were set, the drip secured, the cot-sides double checked and when finally they left the room they went out without turning their backs on their patient.

****

Meanwhile in a hedge bottom four miles away Arthur was sitting the afternoon out in a certain amount of pain. He knew he simply could not continue his journey in this condition nor was he properly aware what his condition was, just that it hurt too much to be able to use that wing and without being able to fly he felt extremely vulnerable. He settled on a plan of returning to the wood before dusk and finding a roost that he could climb into, then he would see how he felt in the morning. At least there was plenty of food there and there would hardly be another days shooting for well over a week. The important thing was to get off the ground for the night, but he didn't want to budge in case someone came back through the wood looking for runners such as he; so he sat there. Gunfire sounded again twice not very far away. A wren came and gave him a thorough inspection with an aggressive and beady eye only withdrawing after some minutes when sure that he offered no threat to her tiny kingdom. Nothing else disturbed him. Sore and stiff he walked back across the grass to the shelter of the wood as the light slowly began to fade. A number of other displaced birds were moving about in a subdued and anxious fashion. He was not alone in his discomfort. A hen pheasant came hurrying up the side of the wood, her beak was slightly open with the effort and as she came close by, Arthur saw the congealed blood that matted the feathers above one thigh. She seemed pre-occupied with her pain and since there was nothing else he could do Arthur accompanied her into the wood. They drank at a puddle near the feeder then Arthur pecked at the yellow plastic knob and stepped back inviting her to help herself. She looked at him warily and helped herself, wobbling as she tried to keep balance whilst eating. The wound looked rather severe. He pecked again releasing more grain but the effort had tired her and she moved off. Arthur hurridly gathered up a meal then followed her into the dusk.

Birds were going up to roost all around them, occasionally quite noisily; but mostly it was just the sound of feathers against branches that gave away their positions. Arthur had rather forgotten his own problem in his concern for the lady. She had arrived under an ash tree, which he presumed was where she normally roosted and she was looking up and crouching ready to go up then giving up. Three or four times she bobbed down but seemed unable to release the effort required. He looked around in the gloom for some easier place. He couldn't fly up either. Not far off was a fallen oak with branches rearing up amongst the hazels there must be a way of scrambling up that. He moved off but she didn't follow. She just sat looking forlorn.

'Come on, you've got to get off the ground to last the night'. 'Oh dear this is very difficult'. Arthur tried cooing deeply and invitingly it was the only attractive noise he could make and it worked. She took notice of him and realized that he wanted to help so hobbled after him. The fallen tree made quite a good retreat. Partially surrounded by brambles and hazel boughs interwoven in the great dead branches it created its own thicket. They clambered up round the roots onto the trunk, then up along a large branch to where it forked and led out into the hazel tops. The hen was tiring now finding balance hard. At the next comfortable fork Arthur stopped and settled, inviting her into the fork where she could sit and lean against the branch. She did so quietly sinking her head onto her breast. Arthur shuffled sideways a bit to be close against her, she trembled and relaxed and went immediately to sleep. Exhaustion rather crept up on him too, the days seemed immensely long or was it just that so much seemed to have happened. This was only his fifth night in an alien guise and yet he was beginning to forget what reality felt like.

Just before he nodded off he heard noises in the undergrowth below, stealthy noises. With straining eyes he eventually made out the dark form of a fox as it passed in front of a clump of pale dead grasses. His senses were wide awake and Arthur was sure that it must have been working at the scent of blood they had left behind. He shivered. That fox would probably feed well tonight there were bound to be others. As if to reinforce that thought his companion trembled again and lurched a little more against him. The night was spent between sleep and wakefulness He could not totally relax because it seemed that as the hours passed he was having to support the injured hen more and more. At last a cold grey dawn started to filter into the wood and with it came some cold grey rain and a rising wind. The fox appeared again as the light was breaking trotting past the end of the ride heading for his daytime shelter.

Despite the cold rain the sounds of birdlife were beginning to fill the wood. Whatever the weather there was still a living to be maintained one couldn't just roll over in bed and expect breakfast to be still waiting at a more congenial hour; except of course for lucky pheasants who had a bin full of breakfast just sitting in the ride below. Two jays were hopping about near the bin waiting for the first pheasant to come and operate the dispenser; something they had not quite worked out for themselves. But at least they knew that if someone else did whatever it was there was a good chance of some easy pickings and it was worth a wait.

Arthur relaxed his pressure against his friend and felt her stir as she adjusted her feet. She opened an eye. It was an inward looking distant eye in which he could read her pain. He sighed. 'Never mind thinking, let's try a little action'. He stood up and shook his feathers a bit sending a double shower down onto the brambles below, then he lent over her and inspected the wound as best he could. The matted feathers had dried and there was really no way of seeing unless one pulled them aside but she was having none of that. She stood up so stiff and unsteady and began' to wobble her way back along the branch. Arthur followed in paternal fashion. When he bumped his wing against a twig he would have jumped and exclaimed with his own pain but since hers was so obviously much more than his he clamped his beak shut and stoically swallowed the expletive. In fact he surprised himself as to how protective he felt. It was not only his own pain that seemed to pale but his whole position now seemed to have taken second place to guiding and protecting this blameless bird. And here was the rub, to Arthur now she was not just a bird but a fellow in distress, which seemed all the more pressing because if he did not assist, no other pheasant would, more likely the reverse. Who of the healthy ones wants a poor sick one in the way? Weaker members of the tribe are always pushed aside in favour of the fit, there is no other law. The relish with which pheasants will pursue each other when artifically crowded is known to all.

The morning passed in attending her as best he could helping at the feeder, scratching up a bit of grit by the old gatepost at the end of the ride and just standing guard while she dozed fitfully under the bracken. Standing in the dripping wood Arthur also knew that he didn't dare continue his journey until he was able to fly properly again. He spent some time trying to assess his own injury and clean the feathers round it. If he stretched in one direction it was no more than sore but if he flexed the wing as if to fly it was excruciating and not to be repeated. For this reason he avoided any confrontations with other cock pheasants. Mercifully there seemed to be a recognized truce around the feed ride and as long as everyone had a few square feet of private space there was no challenging necessary.

No humans appeared that day. The wood and field remained very quiet and peaceful. The two jays were the noisiest members of the community arguing and shouting at each other and throwing a noisy fit when a sparrow hawk thought she would prospect the wood briefly, which at least insured that she went away empty handed. This pleased the lesser inhabitants for all their dislike of jays. By mid afternoon Arthur was beginning to be rather concerned for his charge, she had been sitting hunched up now for a long time and when awake her pale eyelid kept slowly closing. He was annoyed at his helplessness, something he could not become accustomed to. Knowledge of T.C.P. and the efficacy of aspirin was positively useless in these conditions and though he'd lived in the countryside all his life he had no idea if there was any natural remedy to hand. It was a bit late to apply cobwebs and most flowers and vegetation were past and dead even if he knew which ones were likely to be helpful. Arthur had always heard that if a cow was off its food one could titivate the palate by offering ivy; well there was ivy growing on the old gate post they had gritted by earlier. He decided that he had to do something, standing by in sympathy was not enough. So he went off to the post collected a few leaves in his beak and returned, then he pecked them into pieces and laid them in front of the hen pheasant as an offering. Her countenance changed not at all. But Arthur was not to be put off, he next set off down the field edge to where he had remembered seeing a holly bush glowing in a shower of red berries. The difficulty here was getting some berries without causing his own injuries to spoil things but by dint of jumping up and grabbing at a likely twighe ended up with a small cluster of berries, which he bore back in triumph. All he knew was that they were supposed to act as purgatives but since he quite fancied some himself Arthur felt that she might appreciate them too. She did. So much so that he went back for more.

The rain had stopped while he was on his holly berry sorties and by the time the blackbirds started to drink there had been a few watery shafts of sunlight. Going back to the same roost in the oak branches was not so easy. She was stiff and weak and needed to rest after the clamber up the roots onto the trunk. Arthur wanted to make cocking noises as other gentlemen were doing elsewhere in the wood but restrained himself in case that should attract the fox of last night. By slow climbs and long rests they regained their roost. The woodland floor was in deep shadow and the night was fading fast away through the trees. They settled side by side, she trembling all the time now and he feeling much recovered.

Sometime in the night she stopped trembling for when morning came she was stiff and cold.

****

"Please please go away and leave me alone", Arthur

beseeched whatever great spirit was watching to guide the erratic and excitable footsteps of the approaching golden retriever away from where he was crouching and back to its wretched owner who was strolling unconcerned by the hedgerow at least a hundred yards away. Arthur had been walking up the drills of stubble, well out in the field with just the intention of avoiding other beings abroad in the fields. It was really too bad that despite this precaution it looked as if he soon might have to run for his life yet again only this time flight was not an option.

After waking that morning he had been so appalled and upset that he had left the wood straight away and just started walking. Danger or no danger there was no question but that he had to leave. He was surprised at how angry he felt. Marching purposefully seemed to channel his anger. Or was it just frustration trying to get out. One voice inside was explaining away his feelings by saying that it was not unsurprising that knowing what he knew and being unable to communicate with anyone or anything, frustration would be bound to make him angry. The other voice inside was furious at the suffering of his companion and her death. Furious at all creatures around be they human or otherwise that seemed to endlessly abuse each other for their individual gain. It was in this fuming frame of mind that he had not noticed the lady and her dog as soon as he should have.

The retriever was getting closer, it could hardly fail to see him. Suddenly it had his wind. But then something in Arthur burst. As the dog came forward towards him, Arthur arose in fury and with spread wings, tail feathers up he sprang to meet his tormentor, delivering a fierce peck to the soft black nose. He tasted blood and it was good. The retriever let out a shriek and fled off a few yards with its tail tucked down. Arthur rushed after it and in fear and incomprehension the golden retriever rushed headlong back to the safety of his mistress. She meanwhile stood amazed at the sight of a fine cock pheasant crowing loudly, and her lovely big soft dog creeping up to her with bright drips of blood on his nose. Her amazed laughter only increased his discomfiture.

Travelling through this more crowded countryside and having to be extra cautious meant that as the crow flies Arthur took all day to cover two miles. He calmed down after pecking the dog and assessed each new leg of his journey carefully before going forward. Crossing another road took a while for it was not just the traffic that worried him, that he could see; it was more perturbing as to what might be lurking in the hedge on the other side of the road. Then there was a straggling village to circumnavigate. Every time he heard a voice he clapped down tight to the ground until he was satisfied of what the voice was up to.

Lunch was taken amongst a field of outdoor pigs. He crept up on an ark that was home to a sow and piglets and found a nice little creep feeder within easy reach. Others had been here before him. A dead rook dangled from a pole nailed to the back of the ark. 'Hungry visitors to one of the public houses near Tyburn must have felt like this' thought Arthur 'and I don't suppose they were put off eating either'. Inside the ark were sounds of suckling and squeaking, answered by contented grunts. Out of the corner of his eye Arthur could see the sow's nose deep in the straw of her maternal bed. Great sighs and grunts issued forth while he just kept ladling up the pellets to fill his crop. It was only when he felt rather tight across the chest and swallowing was becoming an effort that he desisted. Lack of breakfast had made him inordinately greedy and as he waddled away Arthur began to rather regret his 'piggish' behaviour.

With the urge for fast walking totally evaporated, the afternoon passed in toddling about in the general direction, avoiding any confrontations with anything. It was when he eased himself through a small fir plantation and came out on the wide grassy verge of a little by-lane that he realised exactly where he was. Across the lane was the boundary of his friend Michael's land. Michael who he had last seen only six days ago but who already seemed like past history. Michael's house was but a mile away deep in its own land, well surrounded by woods and trees; and the pheasants hereabouts were plentiful and well fed.

Arthur decided to lodge a while in the vicinity of the house until his wing felt fully capable of use. There was no way he was going to risk the final assault on the hospital without all his feathers. So with a jaunty air he crossed the lane and entered the demesne of the Davenport estate.

CHAPTER 6

Maybe it was his imagination or maybe it was the vistas of large and ancient plantations interspersed with immense majestic parkland trees but as soon as he was entered on the land he felt the stately peace redolent of the passage of centuries. And this was only right and proper considering that previous Davenports had farmed and hunted over this parcel of England since before the first Elizabeth was on the throne. But however stately the place, one still had to keep a beady eye out for passing fox or dog. Particularly a fox for Arthur knew that Michael was a keen supporter of the hunting scene. He stuck to his method of walking across the middle of the fields and taking plenty of time to survey the hedge crossing into the next one.

There was a lot of bird movement to assist him finding the safest route. Pheasants were moving about, along the edge of every plantation and the hedges were busy with finches, tits, and sharp eyed blackbirds. In just over the space of an hour he had arrived within sight of the house. This was a sufficiently huge and elderly pile to qualify for the description of "a seat". It mouldered quietly in a setting of gaunt trees and monster heaps of shrubbery and it was in one of these great heaps of laurel that Arthur thought he could find a very cosy billet for the night, with the added attraction of eyeing the approaches to the front door of Bentwood Hall.

Lights were glowing from the tall windows and the evening gloom was beginning to descend outside. Other bent and hurrying figures were heading for the laurels too so he mingled with them and picked his way into the tangled bushes. It certainly wasn't difficult to find branches to climb up on, the difficulty was seeing where each one led to in the stygian gloom under that canopy of darkened leaves. But by dint of a little shoving and pushing Arthur rose up a score of feet above the ground where he felt secure from night prowlers. It was certainly very cosy, not a breath of wind penetrated and judging by the dry crackle of leaves on the ground not much rain did either. The converse was that there was no view out at all, it was like having the curtains drawn. Arthur slept extremely well.

Morning came slowly in the laurel bush. Other birds had been singing and chattering for quite a while outside before any of the pheasants in the cosy roost felt inclined to come down and start the day. Although he knew his way about the policies at Brentwood quite well, Arthur could not recall the whereabouts of the nearest feed hopper. The simple expedient was to follow other members of the dormitory and let them lead him to his breakfast. Once out on the grass he sipped at the heavy dew, had a good scratch at his chin then extended each wing in turn. The injured one felt much better; he flexed it a bit, yes much improved just painful twinges where before there had been bordering on agony. He didn't quite dare a full drumming of the wings but he felt that was not far off. Strange how powerful were these urges to make one's presence known: he certainly no longer felt like avoiding confrontations with others of his sex. The few times he had let fly and had a good peck at whoever was annoying him resulted in a very satisfactory glow of achievement. Aggression was certainly fun. Arthur was quite amused at himself with this thought. Never in his normal existence had he gone around punching other men on the nose. Nor even considered it. Now he knew he relished the thought and it tickled him quite a lot, and put quite a swagger in his step. In this excellent frame of mind he walked very upright in the wake of the general movement, which was down the drive a bit then left through a wide gap in the shrubbery. The feeder itself was a lot further off than Arthur imagined. Across the tree garden they threaded their way, down by the long wall of the kitchen garden to find it standing in a sea of straw in a clearing in a belt of trees behind the old farmyard.

'Oh well nothing like an appetite to sharpen one up', thought Arthur as he teased out the bedraggled feathers underneath his tail, rather soaked by the dew on the long grass he and his 'friend' had just traversed. There was quite a gathering of birds in the straw all scratching industriously and feeding on what they found. Arthur went over to the feeder since no one appeared to be 'at it' and then realized why. This was not a help yourself job, this was a very grandiose affair, an electrically operated dispenser working on a time clock, which when switched to 'On' whizzed a preset amount of grain out over the straw around it.

"Well blow me, Michael makes his birds work for their dinner! How tiresome". In his rather haughty frame of mind Arthur had not envisaged having to scratch about and spend time over each repast. He was standing there feeling a little put out when there was a click and a whine followed by a volley of wheat rattling all over him stinging quite severely on the back of the head. Enough to make him jump then glower at an unremarkable young cock bird who gave him a quizzical and, to Arthur, an amused glance. He set to work for his food. Next time he heard the click he ducked down and noticed that everyone else did the same. It seemed to be firing on three minute intervals.

An hour of scratching and ducking filled his crop, he then enjoyed a dust bath under a corrugated shelter followed by a long drink from a low galvanized trough - every need was catered for on these premises. Feeling somewhat at a loose end Arthur decided to explore quietly round the house and garden, He felt that one more day of peace and rest would be enough to set him up to continue his journey. Today was a day off but he wanted no more alarms and excursions.

At the far end of Bentwood's extensive gardens was a low lying area with a small stream running through it and here some previous generation of Davenports had constructed a dam and created a small but beautiful lake. It was visible from the house but had always remained a peaceful and undisturbed place. Arthur picked his way slowly across the lawns towards it. A rabbit had been about before him judging by the erratic track left where the dew had been shaken off; they met at the corner of a rose bed where the rabbit had stopped to rub his chin. Neither had anything to say, merely polite curiosity in the doings of the other, the concentration of a rabbit does not last long and after a bit of nose twitching he thought of better things to do than be stared at by a pheasant and hopped off. Arthur enjoyed being by the lake; the sounds were different, more echo; there was plenty to watch and the open lawns gave him safety.

For an hour or more he stood at the waters edge just looking. Some coots were engaged in a furious family argument which rose and fell in intensity; they really were the most vulgar birds. They simply didn't seem to care what others thought or who got in the way. A quiet and inoffensive moorhen jerking its way innocently across the water nearly got mown down in one rather violent part of the argument amidst much splashing and scuttling about. It was while all this commotion was going on that Arthur noticed a movement up on the terrace by the house. A figure descended to the lawn and started to approach. It was Emma. She had no accompanying dog and seemed to be just strolling so Arthur stood his ground. Closer and closer she came. He could see her features plainly now; she was looking at him. He straightened up and fluffed his feathers a bit. She veered from him a little towards a garden seat near the lake's edge and wandered slowly to it, then sitting down drew a pad from the satchel hanging over her shoulder and looked steadily at him. Arthur was at a loss what to do so he did nothing and just returned her gaze.

She smiled and taking out a pencil started to draw. This was all rather flattering. If only there was a way of turning this encounter to his advantage.

'If George married Emma then George would be a lucky man'. He took

two or three slow paces towards her and she responded with a smile that would have dropped him off his perch any day. He took a few more paces, now they were only ten feet apart. He tried one of his most enticing coos but it didn't come out very well and made him feel rather idiotic. She just continued quietly drawing, concentrating but smiling when she felt she had his eye. Arthur paced a little closer to the seat and jumped up onto the other end. If she reached out she could touch him. There was nothing but wonder and pleasure in her eye, no flicker of recognition, what the devil was he expecting – "Oh Mr Beamish how lovely to see you, what can I do to help?"

They must have sat on the seat for twenty minutes with never a word spoken, but the spell was broken by a call from the house. Emma was wanted on the phone. She spoke now.

"I'm sorry but I've got to go." all perfectly normal as if he was just another person. She got up and walked slowly off looking back then quickened her pace and hurried up to the house. Arthur remained on the seat for a little while then realizing that, even if she did some back, the moment could not be recaptured he hopped down and made his way along the path round the lake. He paused now and then to pick a little grit and watch the house but there was no further movement. As he walked on he tried some wing exercises. He was really feeling very much better.

Nothing else of great event happened in the gardens. At one point a cat appeared on the path ahead; it was some way off and showed no evil intent continuing on its way in full view without looking back. Sometime in the afternoon Arthur began to feel peckish again and it was this that urged him to return to the feeder since there really wasn't much edible where he was.

There still seemed to be just as many pheasants scratching in the straw by the feeder as had been there when he wandered off earlier in the day. A large population indeed. The dispenser was still throwing out grain but at larger intervals so there wasn't so much ducking and diving to do but possibly a bit more competition in searching for the grain. Arthur really quite enjoyed this activity. Scratching the straw about with strong sweeps of his feet then a good look to see what was exposed and 'bingo!' a quick peck to grab the grain or piece of cut maize. He surprised himself how accurate one could be in the use of a beak. For the best view of an object it was necessary to turn the head and present one full eye at it, but by trying to look at a grain of wheat with both eyes equally he could almost lose sight of it since there was nearly a blank spot straight ahead. Yet once he had located the morsel he could unerringly pick it up straight ahead. Time after time it worked, it was really quite fun. It was also rather nice to discover that a grain of wheat had quite a strong and delicious taste but that a piece of cut maize was even better, and all this without any chewing or munching around in the mouth.

By now Arthur was in a thoroughly good mood, his injuries were at that comfortably sore stage, not annoying just present giving him the feeling that he had suffered but was recovering fast. Not that he had tried flying; that could wait for he was rather full.

Daylight in late November takes much longer to fade than to arrive and for the birds of the woodland there is more time spent on the roost than awake and active. So for a pheasant that is able to fill his crop with ease and feed twice a day at a feeder, life can be really full of indolence even in the dead of winter. And as Arthur had discovered already, cold temperature did not upset him, the outfit he wore was really most effective. Wet bedraggled feathers were what let the cold in. This evening it felt as if there was going to be a frost. Even with the daylight still pale about the parkland, stars were appearing with a steely glitter. The procession of birds heading for their roosts was not furtive in these conditions, it put one more in mind of villagers heading for a party in the village hall. Upright carriage and cheery recognition by each passer by. Here and there a cock bird drummed his feathers and called out. Chinking blackbirds were going into overdrive. Two tawny owls struck up an extended conversation neither particularly taking note of what the other said, each anxious to be the one who had the last word. Above them all a broken thread of crows were plodding silently towards their communal roost. Going to bed was quite a performance. By now Arthur had reached the laurels where he had spent the previous night. He lingered at the edge of the bushes, looking up towards the house at the warm glowing lights and his good mood took a lurch.

'Bugger it all to blazes' is what actually went through his mind, followed by a chuckle. Even previously he often said things inside that he wouldn't dream of saying aloud. But he chuckled because he realized how much he enjoyed saying things like that and because when things were bad you had to laugh or you'd cry. And whoever saw a pheasant with a handkerchief? which made him chuckle again. Life was really quite hilarious. Tomorrow he would head for the hospital again or maybe just one more day of recuperation. Yes, that was what he needed one more day to be sure he was recovered, for he must have all his capabilities available for the next attempt.

****

Morning came with the grey whiteness of a heavy frost. Through a gap in the curtain of laurel in front of his perch Arthur could see some white faced bullocks across the drive clouded in their steaming breath, and yet their black hairy backs were frosted with rime and seemed as grey as the grass around them. He watched as one deposited a cow-pat and saw the steam rise from it into the cloud of their breath. What a mixture. This prompted him to deposit his own dropping onto the dark branches below, that done he felt ready for action. Hopping down he made his way out of the bushes and stalked proudly through the crackling grass, washing his face in the frost and feeling thoroughly invigorated.

As he had done the previous day he followed in the wake of a number of other birds all making their way to the back of the farm yard in sharpened expectancy of a good breakfast. There weren't many morsels to be picked on the way as an appetiser due to the frost. No worms or slugs were moving above ground. Arthur had a bit of a scratch in a drift of dead leaves looking for something juicy, in the way one digs into a half grapefruit, but met with disappointment despite the dark moist shelter they afforded. All he found was a wizened holly berry and the remains of a dead beetle. What will people say when I tell them what I ate before breakfast, he thought. Then mused in more sombre mood wondering when that might be.

At the feed ride there was considerable activity, all present were scratching away in the straw creating a fresh brown area in all the surrounding whiteness. Arthur joined in. He soon realized that all the searching was not yielding anything to eat and in the minutes he had been there the feeder had not dispensed anything.

"Typical wretched machinery" he grumbled. 'Just when you needed the thing to work most it breaks down, and look at us all anxious and hungry.' He went over to the feeder and inspected it closely. There was frost on the spinning disc so it hadn't produced anything since yesterday evening. The controls unfortunately were out of sight under a cover secured by a butterfly nut. The wiring that was visible ran down to a 12 volt car battery sitting in a box, the connection looked good. He pecked one tentatively - Arthur had never really trusted himself with things electrical - it seemed firm and there was no reaction. 'Probably run out of juice' he thought.

There were about sixty birds scratching away around him augmented by sparrows and chaffinches who were mostly lookers on but had learnt to dart in quick when their larger friends had uncovered something. No one seemed to be having much luck, and no one knew that the keeper had switched the machine off last night after they had gone to roost. After the space of half an hour or more it dawned on them that they would have to look elsewhere and by degrees they began to disperse. Arthur had some knowledge of the layout of the farm and the woodlands. On one side of the belt they were in, lay the old farmyard of Bentwood Hall with the house and gardens beyond, on the other side a large meadow of old pasture sloped down to an open ditch then up again for a similar distance to a mixed deciduous and conifer wood some ten acres in extent. This wood ran on up the slope and over a gentle brow where it became more open and bracken infested before dropping down the slope on the northern side of this roll of land. He had stood at the foot of that far slope many times before, his hands chilling against cold barrels. His heart quickening in anticipation of the birds that would soon stream out across the sky above and straining to hear the first sounds of the beaters and maybe a shout to alert them to the imminent appearance of a rocketing cock.

'Dear me what am I thinking about' Arthur recalled himself to reality. And reality suggested that this popular wood should have a feeder in it somewhere. So thinking he made his way out into the meadow. Others thought the same and they should know. He progressed across the meadow in stately manner, despite some members of his party who scuttled ahead and others who kept stopping and glancing fearfully about. Halfway along the woodland edge was a smartly creosoted gate that lay invitingly open and judging by the number of tracks in the frosted grass must be the way to the breakfast table. The sun was beginning to win its battle for supremacy over the mist and frost haze. Two hundred yards up the slope where the trees thinned and the bracken lay thick, long shafts of sunlight reached down to a large strawed area with a feeder in the middle of it that worked. It was a large one mounted higher and set at five minute intervals.

With nearly a hundred birds, as far as Arthur could make out, this lent for some competition in obtaining one's rightful share. He gravitated to an area where the sunshine had found a way in and made threatening moves at any cock who approached his chosen spot, nobody disputed his right. And when the dispenser whizzed he pecked, swiftly managing to accumulate at least six grains each time. This was not a dignified way of feeding and Arthur found it rather distasteful but hunger is a great leveller and he was darned well going to get his share. In the pauses between times he reflected on how the dispossessed landowners of Russia must have felt when forced to join the bread queues incognito. Fearful of recognition, distressed at their loss of dignity but driven by the common hunger and discovering for the first time that awful law - the survival of the fittest.

The sun grew positively warm and he soon got into the habit of enjoying the warmth, sudden activity when the wheat was scattered followed by more basking and a little scratching. It kept them all happily entertained for well over an hour

It was the shriek of a jay at the bottom of the wood that first raised a few heads. Too wild a cry to be a warning of a fox, more likely warning of a man.

Arthur preened his breast feathers, they did look uncommonly good with the sunlight on them all burnished and reflecting. Then he heard something that made his stomach turn over and the skin down his back tingle - the sound of a reed horn. The signal for the beating line to advance.

What the hell had he been thinking about? Where had he left his brain? Of course it must be Saturday. Saturday the 27th. The day he and George had been asked by Michael to come to Bentwood to shoot. There was no excuse; he could have easily worked it out. Oh you fool. He shouted aloud in his self condemnation and the beaters relished the sound as it echoed down through the trees.

There was general consternation in the feed ride. Those who recognized the sounds melted away into the bracken. Others were unsure and stood erect listening and watching. Feathers flattened, ready for action. Arthur controlled his anger with himself.

'Right, pull yourself together, keep calm. There is a simple answer to the problem'. From experience he knew exactly where the guns would be standing, over the hill beyond, where he might have been right now. Now he knew why the feeder nearer the house didn't work, very clever Michael, very clever.' All he had to do was stay where he was until he was sure that the beaters were doing what he thought they should he doing, namely coming in line up the slope, then either run back through them or fly over them and let them go harmlessly by. 'Relax. Its quite simple'.

****

The tenth baron Davenport was in excellent humour that morning. Frost and sunshine made the countryside look lovely and a sunny day would make all his guests happy. A bit of wind might have improved the shooting prospects but one cannot have everything. He smiled at his own greed. He very much enjoyed his shooting. As he stood looking out across the parkland and all this beauty he sighed at the thought of his close friend Arthur. The last time he had been out with his gun was to Arthur's a week ago and that had ended so disastrously. He had prayed every night that his friend might recover. Helen had told him there was no reason why he shouldn't recover, the doctors said he was physically in good fettle.

A pair of country looking vehicles were coming up the drive. Emma popped her head round the door.

"They're coming", she said

"Good good" Michael replied. He liked George, he liked the idea of George and Emma together, and seeing her excitement at George's imminent arrival he thought that he could actually get quite fond of him.

Helen was coming out for the day too. They had all thought it would be good for her, she enjoyed being out with a dog or stick and if in fact she found it too much too soon then Michael's wife, Elizabeth, would shepherd her back to the house for the day - anyway they would all be in for lunch.

The previous afternoon there had been a council of war between

Michael and his keeper as to how they would conduct the day. There was one drive from kale that they had never done before which had taken some discussion. Then there was a plantation of Douglas fir that had been clear felled and re-planted that spring. As a plantation it had never been worth doing since in the deep darkness beneath the firs hardly any undergrowth survived, but since the felling there had been an explosion of vegetation, and as such had become rather attractive to pheasants and even the odd woodcock. The third alteration they had decided on was the positioning of the guns for the first drive.

So often birds had flown back over the beaters heading for the house and trees around the old farm yard which never got driven through. The upshot of this parley was that they would put four guns at each end of the wood well spaced and good luck to anything that broke away to the sides, meanwhile three or four beaters could come tapping back from the other end to flush the birds somewhere on the crest of the rise where the trees were thinnest. This seemed like an exciting idea, it was always a little dull if things were too predictable.

Shortly after half past nine they issued forth to take their places for the start of the day. Fortified with Gaelic coffee and their own excitement they marched off through the old farm yard and mindful of their host's instructions for relative silence crunched out across the grass with giggling whispers.

George was amongst the first four detailed off to stand along an open ditch that bisected a large old pasture meadow to the right of the track, Emma and Helen went with him. Helen whispered that she would go and stand well back by the trees with Teal to pick up anything if her son could possibly try and connect, at which Emma hissed she would stand close by to embarrass him further! The ground was cold enough to chill the feet but the sun was gaining in strength and really quite warm on their backs. Some of the hoar frost on the branches was beginning to fall, pattering on the crisp leaves below.

The beaters had lined out quietly in front of them and George raised an eyebrow when he realized they were going to be working a line away from the line of guns. Emma pulled a face and shrugged. Then the reed horn sounded and the beating party plunged into the wood.

****

The tapping of sticks on the holes of the trees sounded quite loud as it echoed up the wood. Looking round Arthur realized he was alone in the straw; all his companions had slipped away. If only he could communicate with them, they would be safe. He could start a revolution! As it was he felt rather exposed and crept quietly out of sight into the bracken, still with a view down the slope towards the sound of tapping. But it wasn't from the direction of the tapping that he was surprised. Two hen pheasants right behind him took off in an explosion of sound wings whirring excitedly they rose off up hill, his beak half opened to shout a warning when at the same time his horizon was filled with the face of a fox. Arthur exploded to life too.

There was no question, no time, one wing tip brushed the fox's nose! In the instant he was hurtling aloft going back towards the beaters; a branch struck one wing, the injured wing, Arthur faltered; the pain excruciating. But he couldn't he musn't. 'Keep going'. He was just out above the trees. 'Phew what a relief.' Now he could fly more easily and aim to land at the end of the wood well behind the beaters. His wing was so sore. He set into a glide. Not too far to go now.

But then Arthur got another fright, As he came high over the tops of some tall larch trees that fringed the bottom corner of the wood he saw the men with guns waiting in the meadow beyond. Uncontrollable instinct drove him into a climb. Height; that's what he needed, go so high that no one can touch you. Soar into the sky. Be like a lark.

'Go higher Go higher' a voice shouted in him, his eyes were almost shut with effort and pain. His wing felt like an enormous engine on fire. The cold air rushed round him. Arthur went towering out over the meadow. The sun gold upon his breast, a sight to marvel at.

He flew straight out over his son.

Those that waited in ambush below did marvel at this towering bird, rising higher, seemingly splendid, the epitome of a shooting man's dream - a high bird on a frosty morning. George was excited and tense. He had seen the cock approach just over the trees then the change in flight and now it was coming directly over him. He had practiced his stance, firming the ground under his feet, left foot just forward, good balance, no resting back on the heels. He had swung his gun up a few times before the beginning of the drive, loosening his shoulders so that he was ready, relaxed and poised - or so he thought. A fraction more he waited, then bringing his gun up to the shoulder he swung onto the bird, barrels passing cleanly through the line out beyond the target, keep swinging ahead, arching his back and fusing all in one motion. It was the best shot of his life.

With one choke barrel Arthur's world went red and gold. Pain suddenly swept over him like a furnace. A furnace that turned into a blanket that drew him down. He had lost control, everything seemed dim and far away. The ground seemed to be rising up towards him. Where had the horizon gone? The blanket suddenly tore in half and he hit the turf turning in a cartwheel. Winded and paralysed he tried to focus on the trees but they swam about in huge rubbery waves. Then a big black face was above him. 'Oh Teal, how lovely'.

Teal who had rushed out as soon as the shot was fired. Something he had not done since his training days. But as he approached the prone body in the grass his joyful rush slowed to a wagging creep, with quivering tail tucked in he whined and licked his master's face.

Helen called, wondering what the fuss was about. She was delighted her son had made such a good shot, the first of the day and in front of everyone too, but that did not excuse Teal running in unbidden. Her call was commanding and Teal reacted accordingly. Very gently the dog lifted his 'master' with a velvet mouth and carried him with great care to his mistress. Helen bent for the retrieve and Arthur through the red and gold

saw her anxious face bending towards him and her outstretched hand. As she touched him a warm stream rushed around and carried him away.

****

Arthur Beamish died quite suddenly that morning and at the funeral some days, later the mourners were to recall the final moments beside the grave.

The flint encrusted church was filled to overflowing with friends and neighbours. The psalms and hymns they sang were well known to all and the organist led them at a sturdy and thunderous pace. Towards the end of the service, outside in the churchyard, the vicar paused in silence as Arthur's coffin was lowered slowly into the earth and in that silence everyone heard the distant rumble of artillery on the army ranges far to the south. It was the signal for every cock pheasant in every copse and hedgerow throughout the valley to cry out in answer. Their voices rang loudly round the combes echoing over the bare headed throng among the yew trees and, as all present felt, a fitting salute to the passing of their friend.

A LITTLE ABOUT BARRY

The strange reality that is attached to the hunting and shooting of 'game' is the admiration the hunter has for his quarry. The more noble the creature that one is trying to kill the greater is the regard one holds for it. This holds true for the pheasant.

Early one winter, with the shooting season well under way, whilst on my rounds of the livestock out on the farm, a cock pheasant darted out of the hedge and pecked me on the boot. He did so again the next day as I was unlatching a gate. This became a regular ambush and he began to raise his attack above my boots, he rather hurt my knees so I shoved him off with a gentle kick. Each day he became more bold. One day he must have had a go at the quad bike because I never saw him till I'd run over him! He being somewhat shocked and muddy, I picked him up and cleaned him, whereupon he pecked me for my efforts! Time passed with him daily running beside the quad bike, jumping at my legs and generally being annoying; but only within a certain territory of about 150 yards.

Then came the day he hopped up on to the binoculars I was looking through to check the deer, next jump was onto my head, he crowed with pride at what he thought was a great victory.

From then on, on the morning of a shoot, I picked him up by hand quite easily and put him in a cat basket and left him sitting in it in a hayrack nearby until the beaters had been through his area. I then let him out as we moved off somewhere else. He probably found this rather infra dig but it kept him safe and he became less aggressive and more companiable to the extent of riding with me on the quad bike through his territory – sometimes at high speed! He always hopped off at the same spot and I believe he enjoyed my company as much as I enjoyed his. Two weeks after the shooting season had ended a fox got him. I notified my friends and neighbours of his sad demise and one, Peter Fineman, was moved to write the obituary opposite.

OBITUARY

BARRY P. EASANT

Born Broadoak Game Farm June 2010, died Bush Farm February 2012

Barry Phineas Easant, who has died aged 18 months, was one of Wiltshire's most celebrated and revered characters, much admired by those who were fortunate enough to avoid his clutches.

Born from a shell (hence his initials BP.) Barry was raised in a humble family, by his father Claude, his mother having been outfoxed at a young age. As breadwinner and housekeeper, Claude could ill afford to care for all his children and found it necessary to hedge his bets as to whose nest to feather. Fortunately Barry, being more cocksure than his siblings, was able to fly the nest at an early age.

As a teenager, Barry's dress began to demonstrate increasing flamboyance, such that Claude became somewhat uncertain as to his offspring's sexual orientation. Sadly Claude was then killed in battle and thus prevented from becoming cock-a-hoop at the great heights to which his son would rise as a successful, high flier.

Barry's conduct at school was somewhat unusual: he was noted for a tendency to shun his contemporaries, preferring to consort with adults, whom he recognised as being potentially more useful to him in later years. Indeed this manifested itself by his subsequently setting up home amongst the older, landed nobility. Nonetheless, Barry always maintained an appreciation of his place in the pecking order and, aside from occasional winter Saturdays, he could generally be relied upon to be deferential and indeed affectionate, albeit in his own, somewhat idiosyncratic, fashion.

Whilst he witnessed a number of drives during his lifetime, Barry never learned to drive himself, tending instead to hitch lifts, usually from his landlord, despite having been thrice run over by him, yet seemingly always avoiding more serious injury to himself than he himself afflicted upon his unintentional assailant.

Barry saw action in a number of killing fields but, during the latter part of his life, tended to find himself increasingly boxed in. This sadly encouraged a degree of animosity and aggression, ironically against the one most seeking to protect him. Perhaps for this reason, he is believed never to have married, although he had a keen interest in the birds and fathered a prolific number of offspring, many of whom he outlived.

Barry is survived by a myriad of furred, feathered and clothed neighbours, by whom he will be sadly missed, not least his devoted landlord and mutual antagonist.

Aesop once wrote that "it is not only fine feathers which make fine birds". What more fitting epitaph for "His Nibs", whose only identifiable remains are the odd damaged quill.